Fourth Down Showdown

The Chip Hilton Sports Series

Touchdown Pass
Championship Ball
Strike Three!
Clutch Hitter!
A Pass and a Prayer
Hoop Crazy
Pitchers' Duel
Dugout Jinx
Freshman Quarterback
Backboard Fever
Fence Busters
Ten Seconds to Play!

Fourth Down Showdown
Tournament Crisis
Hardcourt Upset
Pay-Off Pitch
No-Hitter
Triple-Threat Trouble
Backcourt Ace
Buzzer Basket
Comeback Cagers
Home Run Feud
Hungry Hurler
Fiery Fullback

For more information on
Chip Hilton-related activities and to correspond
with other Chip fans, check the Internet at
www.chiphilton.com

Fourth Down Showdown

Coach Clair Bee

Foreword by Jack McCallum

BROADMAN
& HOLMAN
PUBLISHERS

Nashville, Tennessee

0-8054-2092-4

Published by Broadman & Holman Publishers,
Nashville, Tennessee

Subject Heading: FOOTBALL—FICTION / YOUTH
Library of Congress Card Catalog Number: 99-047979

Library of Congress Cataloging-in-Publication Data
Bee, Clair.
   Fourth down showdown / written by Clair Bee ; updated by
Cynthia and Randall Farley.
     p. cm. — (Chip Hilton sports series ; # 13)
   Updated ed. of a work published in 1956.
   Summary: While continuing to lead State's football team
to victory, Chip finds time to help an underprivileged boy
working with him at the drugstore.
   ISBN 0-8054-2092-4
   [1. Football—Fiction.] I. Farley, Cynthia Bee, 1952– .
II. Farley, Randall K., 1952– . III. Title.
   PZ7.B38196 Fo 2000
   [Fic]—dc21   99-047979
                      CIP

1 2 3 4 5 04 03 02 01 00

TO MY PAL
JIMMY LOWE

COACH CLAIR BEE
1956

TO

BOB AND ELLEN STIER

Lifelong Friends
and
Godparents
We have been doubly blessed!

LOVE,
RANDY AND CINDY FARLEY
2000

Contents

Foreword by Jack McCallum, *Sports Illustrated*

1. . . . . . **Extra Help**
2. . . . . . **Shoulder to Shoulder**
3. . . . . . **Starting Quarterback**
4. . . . . . **A Lesson in Strategy**
5. . . . . . **"Wish I Could"**
6. . . . . . **Soapy's Project**
7. . . . . . **Trash on the Corner**
8. . . . . . **An Overdose of Meanness**
9. . . . . . **A Small Price to Pay**
10. . . . . . **Now It's Up to the Kids**
11. . . . . . **The Powerful and Positive Force**

CONTENTS

12. . . . . . **Shakes and Shiners**

13. . . . . . **Big-Time Football**

14. . . . . . **Chicken and Curfew**

15. . . . . . **Yellow-Belt Champion**

16. . . . . . **Soapy Makes the Sports Pages**

17. . . . . . **Crisis and Showdown**

18. . . . . . **Makes a Football Talk**

19. . . . . . **Under the Rock**

20. . . . . . **The Neighborhood Expedition**

21. . . . . . **Friends**

Afterword by Terry Frei, *The Denver Post*
Your Score Card
About the Author

Foreword

IT'S SOMETIMES difficult to figure out why we became who we became. Was it an influential teacher who steered you toward biology? A beloved grandparent who turned you into a machinist? A motorcycle accident that forced you into accounting?

All I know is that in my case the Chip Hilton books had something—no, a lot—to do with my becoming a sports journalist. At the very least, the books got me to sit down and read when others of my generation were watching television or otherwise goofing off; at most, they taught me many of life's lessons, about sports and sportsmanship, about coaches and coaching, about winning and losing.

Also, the books helped me, quite literally, get the job I have now. Over two decades ago, when I was a sports writer at a small newspaper in Pennsylvania, I interviewed Clair Bee and wrote a piece about him and the Hilton books. For some strange reason, even before I met Clair, I knew I could make the story memorable, knew that meeting a legend like Clair and plumbing his mind for memories were going to be magic. They were. I sold the story to *Sports Illustrated,* and, partly because of it, I was later hired there full time.

To my surprise, and especially to the surprise of the editors at *SI,* the story produced a torrent of letters, hundreds of them, all written by closet Clair and Chip fans who, like me, had grown up on the books and never been able to forget them. Since the piece about Clair appeared in 1979, I've written hundreds of other articles, many of them cover stories about famous athletes like Michael Jordan, Magic Johnson, and Larry Bird; yet I'm still known, by and large, as the "guy who wrote the Chip Hilton story." I would safely say that still, two decades later, six months do not go by that I don't receive some kind of question about Clair and Chip.

One of the many fortunate things that happened to me as a result of that story was meeting Clair's daughter, Cindy Farley, and her husband, Randy, as well as others who could recite the starting lineups of Coach Rockwell's Valley Falls teams.

I am proud to have played a small part in the revival of Chip and the restoration of interest in Clair (not that real basketball people ever forget him). It's hard to put a finger on what exactly endures from the books, but it occurs to me that what Clair succeeded in doing was to create a universe of which we would all like to be a part.

As I leafed through one of the books recently, a memory came back to me from my days as a twelve-year-old Pop Warner football player in Mays Landing, New Jersey. A friend who shared my interest in the books had just thrown an opposing quarterback for a loss in a key game. As we walked back to the huddle, he put his arm on my shoulder pads and, conjuring up a Hilton gang character, whispered, "Another jarring tackle by Biggie Cohen." No matter how old you get, you never forget something like that. Thank you, Clair Bee.

JACK McCALLUM
Senior Writer, *Sports Illustrated*

CHAPTER 1

Extra Help

CHIP HILTON'S long legs easily matched the leisurely trotting strides of Fireball Finley, Speed Morris, and Ace Gibbons as they jogged around the outside of the football field. But it took all Chip's willpower to keep from turning the lazy pace into an all-out race. Chip felt like tearing around the newly mowed field and right up the wide concrete steps to the top of the stadium wall. The massive concrete bowl surrounding the striped football field filled Chip with awe, even though the seats were empty.

But they wouldn't be empty on Saturday! Sixty thousand fans would fill those seats, and the vast majority of the fans would be wearing State's red and blue. They would be cheering for the team—and maybe for Chip Hilton. And in Valley Falls, his mom and all his hometown friends would be watching on TV—watching Soapy Smith, Biggie Cohen, Speed, Red Schwartz, and maybe State's new starting quarterback.

Chip glanced at the field. "It's beautiful," he murmured, "just like an emerald set in a band of black gold."

As the foursome made the final turn of the field, Chip's exuberance won out. "Come on!" he shouted. "Let's go!"

Chip's backfield teammates accepted the challenge with whoops and laughs and vied for the lead. Chip lengthened his stride and was soon well out in front. Behind him, he heard the pounding cleats of his pursuers, and then he really began to lift his knees and pump his arms, gradually pulling away. He flashed into the concrete tunnel leading to the locker room and up the steps to the door before he slowed down. Breathing easily, he turned just in time to escape a good-natured swipe from Speed Morris's flailing arm.

"You got the jump!" Speed reminded his lifelong friend. He took a deep breath. "Good thing for you," he smiled. "Next time I'll be the one out in front!"

"Oh, sure!" Fireball Finley grunted, slamming on the brakes and banging into the door. "What makes you think you can run?"

Ace Gibbons eased his heavy frame to a stop. "He's our future backfield—and fast," he gibed. "Didn't you know?"

Morris ignored the late arrivals and laughed. "Everything's all right now, Chip," he said, nodding toward Ace and Fireball. "The tanks have finally arrived. You guys decide to help the managers put away the equipment before coming in?"

The fleet runner was saved from Ace's and Fireball's good-natured roughhousing with the arrival of the rest of State's nearly one-hundred-member varsity squad. In true form, Speed flashed his brilliant smile, snickered gleefully, and darted through the door.

Curly Ralston's "three laps and in" didn't mean that

State's varsity was through for the day. Far from it! Ralston had scheduled a team meeting after the workout, and he was waiting in the team room for everyone to finish showering and dressing. He went right to work on the board, drawing in the plays and shooting questions at player after player. This afternoon's team meeting focused on the offense. Curly Ralston liked to first cover specific teamwide material, and then he would concentrate on either the defense, offense, or special-team players to review what their specific coaches had worked on during the latest practice.

"Nice going," he said at last. "We've been through this time and again, men, but it's impossible to develop offensive coordination and timing in a new system without hours and hours of practice and study. It takes some teams two and often three years to change over, but you've made the change in a matter of weeks."

The determined lips relaxed again. "That's the reason," he continued pointedly, "that Coach Rockwell, Coach Sullivan, and I are convinced that you have the makings of a great team. Not next year or the year after—but this year! Even though many of you are sophomores. Now, get a good night's rest for your classes tomorrow. You looked good today. Real good."

When Coach Ralston finished, Chip hustled for the door. Fireball Finley, Philip Whittemore, and Soapy Smith, all with book bags slung over their shoulders, were right on his heels.

"Late again!" Soapy exploded. "If Coach is gonna keep us practicing late every night, we're gonna be looking for new jobs."

"You can say that again, but don't! There's no time for your silliness tonight!" Whittemore agreed. "Mr. Grayson sure must love football to put up with us."

"Maybe," Chip said. "Maybe he just likes to help guys who've decided to work and go to school."

"Well," Fireball said gratefully, "whatever it is, we're lucky."

Whittemore sighed deeply. "I wish this night were over," he said. "We're going to be swamped. I wish Mr. Grayson would give us some more help on the counter."

"Chip's the one who needs help," Soapy protested. "He never catches up. Inventory, receiving, returns, supplies for the food court, keeping the over-the-counter items stocked for the pharmacy, change for Mitzi, syrups for the fountain, work on the computer and the scanner—"

Fireball groaned. "Please! Enough!" he protested. "I'm tired just listening."

Whittemore was right. Grayson's was jammed when they arrived, and it was mobbed the rest of the evening. Soapy, Fireball, and Whitty dished out pizzas, burgers, fries, shakes, sundaes, and Cokes until they were dizzy. Tonight was especially busy with "Monday Night Football" featuring the Cleveland Browns and the Denver Broncos.

Although Grayson's had started years earlier and still thrived as a pharmacy, the biggest attraction during the school year was the old-fashioned soda fountain and food court. George Grayson had installed a large-screen TV for sporting events, and the location was a magnet for the college crowd.

Chip was on the run all evening too. Keeping up with the stockroom demands of a big outfit like Grayson's made Chip's high school job at the Sugar Bowl in Valley Falls seem easy. His first chance for a break came about ten o'clock. He sank down on the chair by the desk with a sigh of relief. A few seconds later he heard the door open, but he was too tired to lift his head.

EHTRA HELP

"Excuse me, Chip."

Chip leaped to his feet in confusion, the blood rushing to his face. "Hey, Mr. Grayson! I . . . I'm . . . sorry!"

"That's all right, Chip. Relax. I've been watching you for a week or so, and I'm convinced that you need some help—sports or not. I hope you'll be glad to know that I've been running an ad in the paper for a young person to help you in here on evenings and Saturdays."

Chip started to protest, but Mr. Grayson stopped him. "Now, Chip, I know this place, and I believe I could write a pretty fair job description for everyone who works here. You need help, period! OK?"

Chip nodded. "If you say so, Mr. Grayson. But it doesn't seem right. You let me off for practice and games and now you're getting someone to help me do my work. I . . . I— Am I doing OK with my job?"

"Have I ever complained, Chip?"

"No, sir. But—"

Mr. Grayson stopped him. "Yes, Chip, you're doing a great job. But business is growing, and now you need someone to help you. The minimum working age is fifteen, and there will be a lot of applicants to see you tomorrow night. Choose someone who *needs* the job. One you like. They have to be in high school, and depending on their age, they might need a work permit. I'll take care of that.

"This is a busy time for all of us, so I'm adding a couple of people for the counter and food court for evenings and Saturdays too. And, Chip, I realize what a challenge you, Soapy, Whittemore, and Finley face. I think it's great—and by the way, so do lots of others—that you guys can take part in sports, work part time, and still keep up with your studies. Good night, son."

After Mr. Grayson left, Chip sat staring at the computer screen as he tried his hand at creating a job description for his stockroom assistant. As he wrote, he pictured the person he would like to help him. The selection was important to the job, but it was important to him as well. Chip wanted to give the job to someone who helped out at home. He remembered the difficult time his mom had endured after his father had been killed saving a coworker's life at the Valley Falls Pottery when Chip was in middle school. Chip felt an intense desire to help other families.

STOCKROOM ASSISTANT
DUTIES AND RESPONSIBILITIES

GENERAL PROCEDURE:

- Grayson's stockroom contains many valuable items that require careful attention. Details are important to each Grayson's employee.
- The receiving, sorting, storing, data entry, replacement, and delivery of all merchandise to the proper department are the responsibility of the stockroom clerk and the new assistant.
- Every item must be stored in its proper place and entered on the computer so that quantities on hand may be quickly checked, requisitions promptly filled, and orders replenished.
- The key to the stockroom is to be obtained from the cashier, Mitzi Savrill, each afternoon when you report for work and turned over to the stockroom clerk when he arrives.
- The door is to be locked and the key given to Mitzi Savrill for safekeeping if you are sent out of the store on an errand and the stockroom clerk is not working.
- All items and material issued from the stockroom

must be entered on the computer, and the printout must be initialed by the stockroom clerk. It must be checked and signed by the department head when delivery is made. Do not leave the respective department until the printout is signed.

• Pharmaceuticals may only be opened by the stockroom clerk, Mr. Grayson, or the pharmacist on duty.

RESPONSIBILITIES: IN ORDER OF
PERFORMANCE

1. Collect requisitions from each department and enter data into computer.
2. Assist food court supervisor. (Example: Fill all syrup containers and return them to the fountain. Containers must be sterilized by counter/food court supervisor.)
3. Open incoming deliveries and sort carefully so stockroom clerk can check each item against purchase order and shipping receipts.
4. Replace all stock on proper shelves.
5. Make deliveries to department supervisors.
6. Clean, dust, and sweep stockroom carefully.

"That's it," Chip murmured when he finished. "Now for a good night's rest."

The next evening, Soapy exploded into the stockroom and into Chip's thoughts with his usual abruptness. "Big crowd of kids outside, Chip. Just like the movies at the mall on Saturday. Strange thing though. Only two kids came in. I'll send them in to see you one at a time, OK?"

The first applicant was solidly built—about five feet, four inches in height, Chip judged—and weighed about

140 pounds. But the boy was arrogant, and his attitude was almost antagonistic. His keen black eyes swept swiftly around the room and back to Chip.

"What's the job pay?" he demanded.

Chip hoped his smile was friendly. "Here's an application and a pen. First, fill out the front, and then let's talk a little about you," he suggested gently.

"So your name is Tony," Chip remarked as the youngster slid the application across the desk several minutes later.

"Yeah, Tony! Tony Carlara!"

"What does your father do, Tony?"

"He works! What d'ya think?"

"What kind of work does he do?"

"Anything he can get."

"Do you have any brothers or sisters?"

"In our family? That's a laugh. We're a big family."

"Just how important *is* this job to your family, Tony?"

"My family? You hiring all of us? What do they have to do with it? I'm here for me! What I earn, I keep!"

"Don't you help out at home?"

"Me, help out? What for? Why should I? That's the old man's job. I got my own problems and stuff to do."

Chip questioned Tony a little longer and then made notes on the application. "Thanks for coming in. I'll let you know, Tony," he said kindly.

Tony's intelligent eyes probed Chip's gray eyes and held steady. "Who you kiddin'?" he said belligerently. "You ain't gonna hire me." He dropped the pen on the desk, swaggered to the door, and paused with his hand on the knob. "See you around," he said contemptuously. Then he slammed the door, leaving Chip bewildered.

The second applicant was taller and heavier than Carlara but just as arrogant. So the interview didn't last long. Just long enough for Chip to learn that the boy's name was Bucky Husta and that he was Tony Carlara's best friend. After Husta left, Chip waited uncertainly for the next applicant. "Maybe I don't know how to talk to kids who are looking for a job," he mused. "Something's wrong."

Much to his surprise, there were no more applicants. And when he, Soapy, Fireball, and Whitty started back to their rooms in Jefferson Hall, the crowd of boys had disappeared with the exception of Tony Carlara and Bucky Husta. They were lounging just outside Grayson's main entrance. Chip started to speak, but they avoided his eyes and sauntered slowly away.

"That's funny," Chip said.

"What's funny?" Soapy demanded.

"The other kids. Why didn't any of the other kids apply for the job?"

"Beats me," Soapy said. "Who understands this younger generation anyway? C'mon! We've only got ten minutes to get to the dorm. Ralston's probably got cameras on every corner watching us right now to see that we're in Jeff before eleven o'clock."

CHAPTER 2

Shoulder to Shoulder

SOAPY SMITH had long ago arbitrarily appointed himself the "human alarm clock" for his second-floor pals, and he never failed. Every morning, Saturday, Sunday, holiday, or schooldays, Soapy rapped on each door at seven o'clock. Chip and his friends had decided before school opened to set aside two hours for group study every morning. And that meant early rising. No one was excused unless he had a class or the study session interfered with his part-time job.

This particular morning, Soapy herded everybody out of bed and over to the student union cafeteria and then startled his listeners by stating abruptly, "I've been thinking—"

"Wonders never cease! State should declare a holiday!" Fireball observed in an awed voice.

Soapy ignored Fireball's attempt to derail his thoughts, took another sip of milk, and continued. "Chip and I were talking about Mr. Grayson last night, and I figure we ought to do something to show him our appreciation. Chip and I have worked for him for a year now, and he's been great. He lets us off for practices, and every time there's a game he juggles the work schedule and lets us make up our hours later. He's the nicest man I ever met." Soapy thought that over a second and then added, "Next to the Rock."

"I think so, too, Soapy," Fireball said softly. "What's on your mind?"

"Well," Soapy said, "I've been thinking that maybe we could cut down on our breaks and come in earlier on Saturdays and work a little harder." He hesitated and then continued. "Chip's got to have someone to help him in the stockroom, but I think we can get along without anymore help on the counter for now if we *really* put out."

"I'm in on that," Whittemore said, nodding approvingly. "I know I could work a lot faster now that I've been there awhile."

There was a deep, reflective silence as they thought over Soapy's suggestion. Whittemore and Finley had not known Soapy very long, and they must have found this sudden reversal a bit confusing. To them, he had been the comic—except on the football field, of course.

Chip had been a silent observer. Now he took part in the discussion. "Someone should tell Mr. Grayson," he suggested.

"Sounds like Soapy's idea, so it's Soapy's job," Finley said decisively. "Come on. Let's hit the books!"

"Wait! Food! Brain power!" Soapy grunted. "Let me finish these eggs. You don't want that pancake, do you, Fireball? Good. I'll take it off your hands. Pass the syrup, please."

"By the way," Whittemore drawled, as they waited for Soapy to finish breakfast, "how come you don't get

Biggie up in the mornings? He too big for you? Or does he have some kind of special privilege?"

"Yeah," Finley chimed in. "He sleeps more than any six college guys I ever saw. In bed at nine every night and every minute of the day except when he has classes or practice. Must have a sleeping sickness!"

Soapy looked at Chip. "You tell 'em," he said.

"There isn't much to tell," Chip said simply. "Biggie's an engineering student on the co-op program here at State. This semester he's taking fewer classes but has a tough job. He works nights."

"Nights?" Finley echoed. "Doing what?"

Fireball shook his head, and Chip continued. "Well, three nights a week Biggie works in the physical plant facility for the university. He wants to be a plant engineer in Valley Falls."

"Ralston know that?" Whittemore asked.

"Sure," Chip said softly. "But Biggie doesn't talk much about himself."

"C'mon, you guys," Soapy said, rising and gulping down the rest of his milk. "I've got to get busy on psychology. Dr. Edna Smith is my pal. She's gonna give me an A for the semester. I hope, I hope!"

It required all of Chip's concentration to stay focused and absorb his professors' lectures that day. Soapy's attitude about George Grayson had struck a deep chord, and Chip couldn't get the responsibilities of his job out of his mind. Mr. Grayson was a strict disciplinarian, but he had earned the loyalty of all his employees because of his kindness and understanding. Chip had always gone all out to operate the stockroom efficiently, and now he realized that continued success depended on his selection of a good assistant. The behavior of the two applicants the previous evening perplexed him, and he couldn't figure out why none of the others had come in to apply. He was glad when his last class was finished.

Football was a welcome break from classes and work. He hurried down to the gym, changed into his practice uniform, and hustled out on the field. Once there, he forgot all about Grayson's and lectures and concentrated instead on the job of holding his position on the depth chart as State's number-one quarterback. And that took some doing, because his chief rival was the veteran regular, Tims Lansing.

Ralston had shocked more than one loyal State fan when he broke up a veteran team and inserted a number of sophomores in the starting lineup for the opening game against Tech. And Ralston surprised everyone, including the members of his coaching staff, when he had discarded his famous basic straight-T attack in favor of the unbalanced split T.

The seriousness of this last scrimmage before the Brandon game hit Chip with the force of a Biggie Cohen tackle. It was obvious and present in the serious faces of the displaced veterans and in the studied nonchalance of the sophomores who had looked so good in the Tech game.

Sullivan put the players through their stretching warm-up, which was a fast grass drill, and then followed with a series of wind sprints. He then brought them in on a run to circle Curly Ralston.

"Men," Ralston said, "this will be our last contact workout before the Brandon game. Coach Sullivan and the other defensive coaches will run you through our alignments for the Brandon game. Coach Rockwell, offensive coordinator, will run you through the plays in slow motion first and then at game speed. I'd like to go through our basic series before Coach Nelson brings his freshman team over here to demonstrate the defense we expect Brandon to use against us. At the same time, on the other half of the field, our defense will go up against the freshmen simulating the Brandon offense."

The Valley Falls contingent never planned its moves, but at times of importance these friends could always be found shoulder to shoulder. Chip glanced at his friends. Soapy, Biggie, Red, and Speed were standing quietly beside him, and flanking them were two newcomers. Fireball Finley and Philip Whittemore had moved so unobtrusively into the little circle that each was accepted now without a single reservation. Not a word was spoken, but all were gripped by the same thought: *A good showing this afternoon means a starting berth against Brandon on Saturday.*

Ralston read off the depth chart for the offense. "Team A line: Whittemore, Higgins, Cohen, Maxim, McCarthy, Smith, and Brennan. Team B line: Curtis, Schwartz, Morgan, Carlson, Anderson, Clark, and Leopoulos.

"Team A backs: Hilton, Finley, Morris, and Gibbons. Team B: Lansing, Roberts, Cole, and Burk. Everyone else, you're Team C. Play your positions and be ready in case Coach Rockwell calls on you to sub. Let's get busy."

Ralston stood at the line of scrimmage where it met the sideline and gave the signal for the play he wanted run. After six plays for Team A, Rockwell called in Team B and ran it through the next play series.

"All right, Team A, you're offense. Team B, you're defense. Normal line blocking for you but no tackling. We're working on timing. Everyone stay up—no one on the ground! Six plays and then we'll rotate, A off and C on."

It was a hard, bruising workout—much worse than

an actual scrimmage. But no matter how cleverly the coaches attempted to conceal the upcoming offensive play, the other players knew what was coming. That made for a tough workout.

On defense, Chip was playing in the safety position and didn't get in on the actual contact work. But he was glad when Nik Nelson appeared with his freshman team. Not that it made much difference. The big varsity line smothered the freshman interpretation of Brandon's offense. And on the offense, the varsity attack was too strong. Ralston called off the scrimmage after thirty minutes of difficult work.

After showers, the squad assembled in the meeting room, and Ralston went right to work. "I wasn't impressed with our offensive blocking this afternoon," he said sharply. "Frankly, I'm not sure we're all trying to do the same thing.

"It's important that you remember that no matter how opponents change their defensive alignments, it's impossible for them to change our unbalanced line positions. That is the reason we have indicated the holes between our own linemen as the points of attack rather than defensive opponents. Simplified, it means that every player on our team knows exactly *where* we are trying to clear a path, regardless of the moves of the defensive opponents. Are there any questions?"

"Tiny" Tim McCarthy raised his hand. "Coach," he said, "I'm not clear on what to do when an opponent submarines me and ducks under my block. It's almost impossible to move him out of the hole."

"You're right, Tim," Ralston chuckled. "So do it the easy way. Let gravity help you. Fall on him and duck. That will clear the hole, and the back can go right on over the top and through the hole."

"Need a shovel to dig the guy out," Soapy whispered hoarsely.

The whisper brought smiles but no laughs. Ralston didn't go for levity when football was concerned. He glanced sharply in Soapy's direction and continued.

"Now, I'm going to call a name and the number of a play, and I want the player named to call out as quickly as possible who carries the ball and where. OK? All right, Lansing: thirteen!"

Lansing's reply was quick and precise. "Right halfback between right guard and right tackle."

"Brennan: forty!"

"Quarterback to the right of the center, Coach."

"Cohen: twenty-six!"

"Fullback tight to the outside of left end."

"Maxim: three-five!"

It was a cross-up in the method of calling the play, but it meant the same thing. Maxim reacted promptly. "Left halfback off right tackle!"

"Whittemore: Forty-eight!"

"Hil—" Whittemore caught himself. "Quarterback wide around left end, Coach."

There was a pause, and it was clear that State's varsity had devoted a lot of time to learning its plays. Ralston nodded approvingly. "Nice going, men. Now, one more thing. Coach Sullivan has diagrammed some of our defensive sets. I'm sure you can determine the proper signals. Coach Sullivan will hand them to you on your way out. Everyone meet with your specialty coaches before leaving the room."

Soapy was the first person out the door. He grabbed the sheet of paper from Jim Sullivan and waited impatiently for his Grayson's coworkers. "C'mon," he urged impatiently. "It's five minutes to six. We're gonna have to run to make it. Besides, I gotta tell Mr. Grayson we can handle the counter without anymore help."

Chip took the lead and set a fast pace, but it was five minutes after six when they reached the store. And there, just outside the main entrance, Chip was surprised to see Tony Carlara and Bucky Husta. The two boys pretended to be engrossed in the window display, but when Chip halted, they walked quickly away.

"Well, what d'ya know?" Soapy commented. "Your pals are back."

During the long, busy evening, Soapy managed to get back to the stockroom to tell Chip about his talk with Mr. Grayson and to report on the continued presence of Tony Carlara and Bucky Husta.

About seven o'clock, a high school girl walked past Tony and Bucky without them giving her a second glance. She paused inside the doorway as if unsure what to do next, but then she moved toward the counter and faced Soapy.

"What can I prepare for you this evening, young lady?" Soapy smiled.

"Nothing really. I'm here about the job," she replied quietly.

Without thinking, Soapy blurted, "You're a girl!"

Leah Cahill blushed and laughed nervously. "Is that a problem?"

"Nope, not for me!" Soapy grinned, thinking about Chip. "Go right through those doors, and you'll find Chip Hilton. He's the one you have to talk to about the job."

Chip, working on the computer, looked up from the screen as a quiet voice asked, "Are you Chip? I'm here about the job."

As the two talked, he quickly learned that Leah was a sophomore at University High School and a solid

B student. Her mom had passed away when she was ten, and she lived with her dad and twelve-year-old sister. The only job she had ever had was baby-sitting. She liked computers and had played in the summer soccer program.

Leah told Chip her high school counselor was encouraging her to think about going to college. She wanted the job to start saving money since funds would be even tighter at home if she went to school.

After Leah left, Chip made notes on her application. She seemed sincere and had all the qualifications Mr. Grayson mentioned. Then he wondered how many students he should interview before making a decision. He went outside several times to see if there were more applicants and to question Tony and Bucky. There weren't anymore applicants, and each time he neared the door, Tony and Bucky disappeared quickly.

It was the same Friday night and Saturday morning. Tony and Bucky were right on the job, but not a single other applicant showed up. Chip tried in vain to catch the two sentries and would have regarded the strange game as good fun except for his urgent need for help.

"I'll settle this tonight," he assured his friends when they started for the stadium. "If I have to chase those two all the way to Valley Falls!"

CHAPTER 3

Starting Quarterback

CHIP WAS the first player suited up. He concentrated on his uniform, fussing with the sleeves of his jersey and his shoulder pads. Then he tried on his helmet and adjusted the chin strap. Next, he unlaced his right shoe, took it off, carefully inspected the kicking toe, and laced it on again. All during the preparations, he was conscious of the old familiar knot in his stomach and the tight feeling in his chest. But Chip wasn't the only player in the room who was having uniform trouble. Most of the sophomores were experiencing the same difficulty.

Murph Kelly, State's wise trainer, recognized the signs and began chattering away. "We're breaking a three-year jinx this afternoon, everyone. Mark my words! We've lost the second game on our schedule for the last three years, and we're changing that this afternoon!

"Come on, Smith! Stop playing with those shoulder pads and put them on. What d'ya think this is, a stand-up comedy act?

"Oh, no, you don't, McCarthy. Take off that sock and get those ankles taped. Every player gets his ankles taped by my training staff for practices, scrimmages, and games. You know that! Besides, it's Coach's orders!"

It seemed hours later when Chip found himself on the field. A quick glance showed that the stadium was packed clear up to the top row. Then the stretching, warm-up drills, and kicking and passing were over, and he was standing in front of the bench with the starters, restlessly kicking his cleats at the grass and trying to listen to Coach Ralston's last-second instructions.

Captain Mike Brennan charged into the circle, pulling on his helmet and rasping, "We kick! We kick!" Chip trotted out on the field while the State fans rose as one and cheered the appearance of the team taking its place on the field.

Back in position for the kickoff, Chip tried to concentrate on the ball. But it was swaying from side to side on the kicking tee, and his legs felt as though they were made of straw. Then a whistle shrilled, and Chip raised his arm as he lurched toward the ball. At that precise instant, sudden strength and power flooded him, and the ball steadied and looked as big as a pumpkin. Chip drove forward, figuring he could kick a hole in the ball, and he tried to do just that.

It was a good kick, angled toward the right, and it carried to the goal line. But Brandon University quickly demonstrated that State University was in for a busy afternoon. The five tall, rangy forwards sped back across the restraining line and formed in front of the receiver almost as soon as he caught the ball. The ballcarrier picked up the wedge and kept in its shelter as far as the thirty. There, he broke out into the daylight to his right and angled for the sideline.

Biggie Cohen broke the wedge on his side, and Whittemore should have made the tackle. But Whitty overshot the mark, and the runner slipped past him and darted past the forty-yard line—away, it seemed, for a sure touchdown. Chip had followed the ball and was caught on the wrong side of the wedge. But Speed Morris, playing safety on the kickoff, took care of the desperate situation, cutting the runner down on the midfield stripe with a beautiful driving tackle that brought a roar of relief from the home stands.

The State defense charged onto the field, and Brennan immediately called his team into the defensive huddle. "Forget it," he said crisply. "Settle down now. It won't happen again! Remember what Coach Sullivan said about their passing. They'll open up now! Try for a quick score!"

When play resumed, Brandon's quarterback faked a pass downfield and then threw a hard, fast peg to his left halfback in the right flat. Fireball had followed the receiver out in the flat and gambled on an interception. But he was a step too slow, and the speedy receiver gathered in the ball and cut laterally toward the left. It was amazing how quickly his downfield blockers formed.

Brennan, backing up the other side of the line, came across quickly, but he met the full impact of the blockers and didn't have a chance. Chip had picked up the Brandon left end who had outdistanced Gibbons, and Ace turned back just in time to bring the runner down on the thirty-yard line.

Brennan called for the 5-3-3 defense in the huddle, and Chip hurried back to the twenty-yard line. Chip was now gravely aware that Brandon was a top-flight opponent with a fast and determined line and a lightning-fast backfield. The visitors crossbucked for six quick yards, reversed inside Higgins for five more, and it was first and ten on the State nineteen-yard line. The Brandon fullback hit the strong side tackle for three and came right back up the middle for five more. An end-around play carried to the State five-yard line, and it was first down and goal to go. Brennan looked to the sidelines as substitutes were coming in for State.

Ralston sent Schwartz in for Higgins, Curtis for Whittemore, and Cole for Morris, while the "hold-that-line" chant of the home fans boomed across the field. The chant became a roar, and Chip could scarcely hear the Brandon quarterback calling his signals. Then the keen-eyed passer spotted his lanky right end leading Boots Cole toward the right corner of the end zone and rifled a fingertip pass over Cole's head. It was a touchdown! Seconds later the Brandon kicker booted a perfect placement to make the score Brandon 7, State 0.

State's fans had the right idea and came right back with it. "We want a touchdown! We want a touchdown!"

Chip's favorite play was to run back a punt or a kick-off. It gave him the same thrill that he experienced in baseball when he got hold of one and sent it winging over the fence for a home run. "Now's the time," he told himself.

The thump was clear and piercing. The ball came spinning high in the air and right at Chip. He had to wait for the ball on the five-yard line, and the fast Brandon tacklers were at the fifteen when he gathered it in. The State wedge was far ahead, and Chip had only the blocking of Fireball, Boots Cole, and Ace Gibbons to meet the swarm of tacklers. They weren't enough. Players on both sidelines could hear the crack of pads as the ballcarrier was taken down. Chip was buried on the twelve-yard line under a pile of eager visitors.

Chip was shaken up on the play, but he leaped swiftly to his feet and hurried back to the huddle. "All right, guys," he said sharply. "Twenty-one on four! Let's get a good drive started!"

Up to the line and on the fourth number, the State center gave Chip the ball with the sharp plunk that always filled him with confidence. He pivoted to his left, faked a handoff to Cole with his right hand, and, holding the ball behind his back with his left hand, slipped it to Fireball. It was clever hidden-ball strategy, and Fireball exploded into the line and out and up to the twenty before he was brought down. State's fans roared approval for that bit of sleight-of-hand, and it gave Chip a big lift. He came right back with another straightaway play.

"One-four on three! Let's keep it going!" Chip said, winking at Ace Gibbons. "Give us some help, Biggie and Wally!"

Ace Gibbons played hard and fast, and he hit behind the blocking of Cohen and Wally Curtis like a mad bull. His plunge was good for six yards and a first down. Chip kept alternating Fireball and Gibbons, and as they ripped off gain after gain and first down after first down, his confidence returned.

Then disaster struck. Chip sent Cole over right tackle after faking to Gibbons. Boots made the difficult up-and-back stride and dashed between Maxim and Schwartz with precision but fumbled the ball. Brandon recovered on its own twenty-five.

It was hard to take, but Chip pulled Cole to his feet and whacked him on the back. "My fault, Boots," he said. "It was a bad pitch to you."

"Come on, guys!" Brennan urged. "We'll get it back!"

State had the determination and fought tooth and nail. But Brandon University controlled the ball, stopped

State's running attack cold, and drove relentlessly into State territory time after time. Chip's kicking was magnificent, but the visitors kept knocking at the door and finally broke through for their second touchdown. The score at the half was Brandon 14, State 0.

Sitting in the locker room, Chip leaned forward, deep in thought as his hands gripped the bench. He wasn't moving. He stared at the floor as if he were tired out and giving his arms, legs, and muscles a much-needed rest. But the rigid position of his body testified otherwise.

Inwardly, Chip was tearing himself apart. His first-half performance had been awful. He'd been foolish to rest on the laurels he'd earned the previous week, he told himself. One game didn't make a season. Instead of playing his own game and mixing up his plays and concentrating on winning the game, he had tried to make each of his backfield teammates look good. He had forgotten all about his role as team leader in the quarterback position.

Coach Ralston believed in giving his quarterbacks responsibility on the field. He schooled them in this type of attack in the practice workouts and strategy sessions and let them do their own play calling in the games. Chip appreciated the freedom, but he was far from happy with his selection of the plays for that first half. He had fallen for Fireball's exuberant confidence and used the blockbuster too often. It had been the same with Ace Gibbons. As the only veteran in the starting backfield, Ace was entitled to every consideration, but Chip had leaned over backward. Now he was paying for his weakness—and so was his team.

Yes, that's what it is, he thought. *Weakness!*

A quarterback's job was to direct his team to victory, and it was of little importance who carried the ball, made the touchdowns, or got the cheers.

STARTING QUARTERBACK

Curly Ralston's cool, penetrating voice broke into Chip's thoughts. "All right, men. Give me your attention."

The marker, incongruously fragile in the broad hand of the coach, glided across the board. "Whittemore! Back in at end!"

Chip's eyes flickered toward Whitty. The big junior college graduate had really come into his own in the Tech game. Whitty had won the all-important opening game almost by himself. With ten seconds left to play, Whitty had faked a block and then reversed around behind Chip on a modern version of the old, time-worn Statue of Liberty play. It was good for a touchdown and the victory. Whitty belonged! He was six-four and weighed 210 pounds, and he could move his rangy frame like a running back. Wally Curtis was an experienced senior and almost as big, but Whittemore was better by far.

"Cohen! Rush the passer! We didn't get across the line fast enough nor far enough in the first half."

Chip followed Ralston's glance. Biggie Cohen was six-four, 240 pounds of steel, and as quick as a tiger. Joe "Troubles" Morgan was as tall but fifty pounds lighter. The veteran was good, but he couldn't play left tackle like Biggie. Nobody, but nobody, on this team or any other, could measure up to Biggie. Chip glanced at his hometown friend again. Biggie hadn't moved a muscle.

"Anderson! You're fast enough and small enough to slip through those holes in the Brandon line. I want to see you in Brandon's backfield on every play!"

Chip liked Eddie. The sophomore guard was five-nine and weighed only 185 pounds, but he was a scrapper. Coach Ralston liked that in a football player. Fast too! But "Tiny" Tim McCarthy weighed 245 pounds and was as fast. On the defense, Tiny Tim was the best Chip had ever seen.

"Brennan! Strengthen our pass defense. Their passing is making us look silly!"

Chip evaluated State's rugged captain. Mike was an even six feet in height and weighed 205 pounds. He was a member of the junior class, but when it came to football, Mike was a Ph.D.

Chip's eyes flashed toward Stavros "Bebop" Leopoulos. Bebop was as big as Brennan, but there the comparison ended. Mike Brennan was a hustling, fighting leader, an expert center, and a raging lion on the defense. Mike was a cinch for all-conference, maybe all-American.

Ralston's voice bit through again. "Clark! You heard what I told Anderson. Same goes for you! Except when you're playing in the secondary against passes. Then I want to see you cover the hole down the middle like a blanket."

Chip didn't agree on that selection. Ralston knew best, of course. But when it came to pass defense, Soapy was the greatest. Clark had been through the mill, but Soapy had a nose for interceptions and he was bigger and tougher.

"Maxim! Crash that line more, Joe. Hit that big end at the line on your way after the passer. He's their best receiver."

Chip agreed on that selection, all right. Who wouldn't! "Silent" Joe was only a sophomore, but he had nailed down the right-tackle spot from the very first day of practice. Joe was six-two, 195 pounds, and a deadly blocker and tackler. He never gave his opponent a second of rest on the offense or defense. Joe was good enough for any man's team.

"Higgins! When you're in, I want you to crash too! Get those arms up on passing situations! Use your height to knock the ball down the passer's throat!"

STARTING QUARTERBACK

Larry Higgins reminded Chip of Sky Bollinger, State's freshman basketball center. Larry was six-five and 180 pounds. "He'll be all over the Brandon passer this half," Chip breathed to himself.

Time was running out, and Ralston's words came faster and faster.

"Cole! Gibbons! Finley! Lansing! I want to see every receiver covered on every play. Check with one another and then check again. Don't fall for the fake slants. Watch the ends. If they come out of the line fast and head upfield, they mean business. Don't let anyone get behind you. Understand?

"All right now, let's sum it up! Good defense. A fast, hard-charging line deep in the Brandon backfield. Smart covering of pass receivers! Mike! Use a five-man line when you smell a pass situation. Try the umbrella pass defense! And check coverage of every receiver.

"Now the offense! Lansing! Mix up your attack! Don't gamble. We've got lots of time. Thirty long minutes. Open 'em up with passes and then strike on the ground. When they tighten up the line, hit through the air!

"Mike, we'll be receiving! We need the ball! All right, men. Let's go!"

Chip didn't have much time to think about Ralston's second-half backfield right then because every player in the room surged around Ralston in an attempt to join in the team clasp. But, mobbed and pushed as he was, he didn't forget that he had just lost out as State's starting quarterback.

CHAPTER 4

A Lesson in Strategy

STATE IS a big-little university. Students never get "lost" on the campus or in the classroom, and the professors make it a point to know their students. The sports fans are like that too. They remain loyal—win, lose, or draw! Now, they rose to their feet en masse and expressed their faithful support with a cheer that exploded and held its volume as the Statesmen charged out onto the field and readied for the kickoff.

Chip headed for a seat on the bench and then allowed himself to think about the second-half backfield. He started with Tims Lansing, State's veteran quarterback. Lansing was six-one and 185 pounds, give or take a little, but Tims was three years older and had two years of big-time football experience under his belt. Chip knew he was a better passer, kicker, and runner than Lansing. But he knew, too, that a quarterback had to have a lot more than just football skills.

"It's my own fault," Chip whispered under his breath.

A LESSON IN STRATEGY

"Why did I let sentiment influence my judgment? The coach gave me my chance, and I screwed it up—before sixty thousand people! A great time to freeze up! I'd better concentrate on Tims and learn something about leading the offense."

Soapy was disgusted. He threw a towel over his helmet and peered angrily out at everyone in sight. Then he jabbed a heavy elbow in Chip's ribs. "Don't be a chump," he growled reproachfully. "This is for keeps! Carry the ball yourself once in awhile. And pass and kick the way you should, and the way you know. Forget those other guys! OK?"

Chip nodded grimly. "Don't worry," he promised. "I'll never make *that* mistake again. That is, if I get another chance."

"You'll get another chance," Soapy muttered. "Don't mess it up!"

State was out on the field now, and Chip scanned the other backs. He'd sure go along with Ralston when it came to Fireball. The big fullback was the hardest running back Chip had ever seen. Finley could break through a hole in the line and be out in the open before anyone knew he had the ball. Furthermore, Fireball was six feet in height and weighed 210 pounds, all of which was muscle. He was almost as durable as State's concrete stadium.

Gibbons at right halfback could have come out of the same mold. Ace had been State's regular fullback the year before, but he had been shifted to right halfback to make room for Fireball.

"We've sure got 'em," Chip breathed, thinking of the formula for a winning college team. "Two big tackles and a fullback!"

Soapy's head swung around. "What did you say?" he demanded.

Chip shook his head. "Nothing, Soapy. Just thinking out loud." He focused his eyes on Boots Cole. Boots was a senior, five-eleven in height, and weighed 165 pounds. He was a good, steady halfback. But Chip preferred his high school teammate, Speed Morris. Speed was about the same size at five-eleven and 170 pounds, but Speed was a streak of lightning with the ball. Once past the line, he had what it took to go all the way. He had a change-of-pace step that had bewildered many a sure tackler.

Chip found himself on his feet then as he joined the bench warmers in cheering the players on the field. The crowd noise was deafening as Brandon's wave of gold-and-black-clad players started slowly and then surged down the field in swift pursuit of the spinning ball. The second half was underway!

It was a fairly short kick, and Fireball took the ball on a dead run. Heading straight up the middle, the block-buster sprinted past his own blockers and burst through the tip of the wedge and out in the open. Fireball's speed was so blinding that one tackler, then another, and finally two more went spinning off his pounding knees. Then the kicker missed him completely, and it looked as if he might get clear for a touchdown. But the Brandon safety saved the day for the visitors with a desperate shoestring tackle that flipped Fireball high in the air and down on the State forty-five-yard line. So, on the first play of the second half, the home fans had something to cheer about. The thunder of approval was so deafening that Lansing was forced to shout the signals in the huddle.

The cadence of Lansing's voice as he hurried the team out of the huddle and sent Gibbons tearing through right tackle seemed to complement the momentum of Fireball's mad dash. Gibbons's plunge was good for five yards and placed the ball on the midfield stripe.

A LESSON IN STRATEGY

"Concentrate on Tims's strategy now," Chip muttered to himself. "Don't miss a single thing!"

Tims shocked Chip right off the bat. On second down, with five yards to go, Tims shot a high spot pass to Whittemore right over the line. It was a surprise play, and it clicked for four yards. Boots Cole was hurt on the play, and Speed was out on the field before Ralston could say "Morris!"

Murph Kelly helped Cole to the bench, and when time was in, it was third down with a yard to go. Chip and every fan in the stadium knew what the next play would be: Finley on the handoff in a hard, diagonal lunge into the line! But Lansing crossed up Chip, the fans, and Brandon's defensive wall as well. He sent all 170 pounds of Speed Morris flashing straight through the left tackle slot, and the Valley Falls flash went all the way to the Brandon thirty-five before the surprised secondary could bring him down.

Brandon called for time then, and Chip thought it over. He was learning fast. Lansing had used his running back on a quick-opening play through the *weak* side tackle instead of sending one of his heavy-line plungers, Fireball or Ace, through the *strong* side of the power zone.

When time was in, Lansing fooled Chip once more. He used Speed again! He sent the speedster scampering through right tackle on a cross buck with a trap on Brandon's left tackle.

Speed broke into daylight and went all the way. Biggie Cohen made the key block on the ten-yard line, mowing the Brandon left halfback down with a crash that knocked the unfortunate visitor clear out of bounds.

Chip was on his feet, cheering and mulling over this bit of strategy, when an elbow crashed into his ribs and nearly knocked him back over the bench.

"Get goin'! Get out there!" Soapy hissed, pushing him toward the field. "You deaf? Ralston's sendin' you in to kick the extra point. What's the matter with you?"

Chip quickly fastened his chin strap and cast a frantic glance at Ralston. The big coach was looking right at him, and that was enough for Chip, right or wrong! He tore across the field, thumping Lansing on the back on the way. "Great, Tims!" he shouted. "Great!" And Chip meant it with all his heart.

With Speed holding, Chip booted a perfect placement and started back up the field, his spirits revived. He'd show Coach Ralston a little of Chip Hilton's brand of field leadership. He glanced at the scoreboard: Brandon 14, State 7. It didn't look so bad now. State was back in the ball game!

Brandon elected to receive, and Chip gave the boot all he had. But he got a little too far under the ball, and it went high in the air, spinning end over end and down to the Brandon receiver on the ten-yard line. Mike Brennan made the tackle on the fifteen, and Chip turned to drop back to the safety position. Then he saw replacement Wynn Burnett running in his direction. "Oh, no," he breathed.

"Sorry, Hilton," Wynn said, jerking his thumb toward the sideline. "Nice boot!"

Chip heard the "Yea Hilton!" from the State cheerleaders, but the ache was back in his chest. Soapy and Red and the rest of the bench gave him a standing ovation and high-fives as he hustled past Ralston. This time he heard the coach.

"Nice going, Hilton," Ralston said. "Thanks!"

Soapy greeted Chip like a long-lost brother. "That's more like it!" he gritted. "Now you get ready! Ralston's gonna send you in the next time we get the ball! Wait and see!"

A LESSON IN STRATEGY

But Ralston didn't.

Brandon's quarterback and center missed the snap exchange, and the ball squirted away and was quickly covered by "Tiny" Tim McCarthy at the State twenty-three yard line. Coach Curly Ralston sent Tims Lansing in to lead the offense.

Lansing crouched behind center and team captain Mike Brennan to receive the snap. The first play from scrimmage developed as planned. Tims faked the hand-off to Morris, cutting over right tackle—the same play Speed had earlier turned into a touchdown. The defensive line momentarily froze as Tims whirled and pitched out to Ace Gibbons, who was dashing toward the left side of the Brandon line. Ace tucked the ball under his arm and turned the corner for six yards before being shoved out of bounds by the Brandon defensive secondary. Chip kept his eyes fixed on every move Tims Lansing made. The veteran quarterback had taught him a lot in that earlier touchdown drive. Now he'd let Tims teach him some more.

With second down and four to go, Tims sent Morris through the right side, hoping to fool the Brandon front line once again, faked the pitch to Gibbons on the repeat pattern, and kept the ball himself. Tims sprinted for the right sideline.

An explosive roar from the stands told the story. Lansing was around the corner of the defensive line! State blockers appeared in front of Lansing as he tore straight down the sideline toward the Brandon goal line before he was knocked out of bounds near the ten-yard line.

Chip was cheering the wonderful run and thumping Soapy on the back when he suddenly realized the stadium had quieted. Lansing hadn't gotten up!

"No," Chip cried. "Oh, no! Not after that play!"

Lansing was surrounded by the officials and a knot of players from both teams now, and a dead silence hung over the stadium. Ralston and Rockwell had nearly reached the scene when Murph Kelly stood up and beckoned. There was a short consultation, and a moment later Tims was carried toward the runway on a stretcher by two of Murph Kelly's assistants. Ralston, team physician Dr. Michael Terring, and Murph Kelly followed. Rockwell came back, shaking his head and nodded to Chip.

Then, as the little group accompanying Lansing turned into the tunnel leading to the locker room, the stadium came to life and cheered the great quarterback to the skies. Soapy was gripping Chip's arm and shaking him. But all of Chip's joy had vanished. He didn't want to capitalize on Tims's misfortune.

Brennan's keen eyes measured Chip when he trotted into the huddle. "It's all right, Chip," he said understandingly. "We know how you feel. Let's just get this done for Tims! Right now!"

State didn't win it right then. But the Statesmen did tie it up. Brandon's line and secondary defense had tightened up in expectation of State's power offense. But Chip took a page from Lansing's book and raced out to the right behind his backs, as though for an end run. Five yards from the sideline he slid to a stop and hit Whittemore with a hard, waist-high pass. Chip put everything he had into that throw. He was determined. No Brandon player was going to hold that toss, even if he did get his hands on the ball!

Whittemore grunted when the ball plugged into his belly, but he held it and bulled his way to the four. On the next play Chip avoided the obvious as he seemingly used the same play. This time, however, he handed off to Gibbons just before faking the same pass. The big back circled back and tore around the left side of the line without blockers—a naked reverse. Ace was hit at the line of scrimmage, but he bucked and fought and forged ahead to fall across the goal line for the score.

State's cheerleading squad tumbled and jumped along the sideline. Then, when Chip booted the extra point to tie the score at 14-14, the air over the whole stadium filled with red-and-blue confetti. And the happy fans were still at it when Chip lined up behind the ball for the kickoff.

Chip's spirits soared. It was a new ball game! He met the ball just right, and it cleared the end zone, bounded on the track, and rolled clear to the stadium wall. It was a mighty kick and indicative of State's new strength. Before Brandon could put the ball in play, the third quarter ended, and the teams changed goals.

Rockwell sent Smith in for Clark, McCarthy for Anderson, and Schwartz for Higgins. The newcomers were eager and fresh, and the State forward line now averaged more than two hundred pounds per man. But it wasn't the weight that made the difference. It was the spirit and the hustle and fight the newcomers displayed. Brandon put the ball in play on the twenty-yard line and couldn't do a thing. State's weight and determination began to tell, and the visitors were forced to punt after three weak offensive plays.

The Brandon kicker got away a high, tricky punt that carried to the State thirty-five. Speed Morris was surrounded and called for a fair catch. The clock showed twelve minutes to play, and Chip was sent back in to lead the Statesmen. After gaining two first downs, their drive stalled and they were forced to punt.

The State defense held again, and the visitors couldn't gain a foot. Brandon punted to midfield, and three downs later, Chip returned the compliment. This time, the ball rolled out of bounds on the visitors' three-yard line. Two Brandon line thrusts were piled up without the gain of an inch, and its third-down pass attempt fell incomplete. When the kicker dropped back to punt, he was standing deep in his own end zone.

Kicking from the end zone is tough at any time. But when the game is drawing to a close and the opponents are fighting and charging and rushing every pass from center, it's plain suicide. This time, the Brandon kicker was lucky to get the ball away. It slithered off his foot, barely missing the charging State line, and went spinning out of bounds on the Brandon eighteen.

So, the exchange of punts had paid off, and Chip chalked up another bit of thanks to Tims Lansing. The ball rested on Brandon's eighteen-yard line, and it seemed to Chip that sixty thousand fans were chanting in unison, "We want a touchdown! We want a touchdown! We want a touchdown!"

Brandon was far from through. The visitors still had plenty of fight. State did push the ball to the Brandon six-yard line on a short pass to Whittemore and two line plunges by Fireball and Gibbons. It was first and goal to go, and it looked like a sure score. But the visitors, fighting like madmen, knocked one of Chip's high end-zone passes away from Whittemore, hit Gibbons behind the line for a three-yard loss when he slipped, and held Finley to a four-yard gain off right tackle. That made it fourth down and goal to go, with less than a minute to play. It was now or never!

Chip had called his plays with an eye to a winning field goal, and when State formed its huddle back on the

A LESSON IN STRATEGY

fifteen-yard line for the last play, the ball was almost in the center of the field. Mike Brennan held out one hand for the team clasp and patted Chip softly on the helmet with the other. There was no need to call the play.

"We'll hold 'em, Chip!" Mike promised. "Take your time."

There really wasn't much to it. State's big line held like a stone wall, and Speed took care of the rest, handling the ball perfectly and spotting it just right. Chip could have kicked that one with his eyes closed.

The clamor from the stands dwindled to the rumble of distant thunder just before Chip booted the ball between the goal posts. Then the rumble exploded into a deafening roar as the ball carelessly tumbled down the net suspended between the goal posts and into the waiting arms of a team manager.

Chip was mobbed by his teammates, and Rockwell had a tough time keeping the rest of the squad off the field. There was time left for one play, but Chip kicked the ball over the end zone again. Brandon had to settle for a long, incomplete pass from the twenty-yard line, and then the game was over. The final score: State 17, Brandon 14.

CHAPTER 5

"Wish I Could"

CELEBRATIONS ERUPTED when the game clock showed 00:00! Students spilled out onto the field, mobbing the victorious Statesman players, coaches, and managers. Chip was separated from his teammates by a solid wall of old grads.

"Hey!" one shouted. "It's number 44! It's the quarterback!"

"That's Hilton! He won the game!"

"Way to go, Hilton!"

In just moments Chip was the center of a milling crowd of cheering fans who persisted in trying to get him up on their shoulders. Smiling all the time, Chip kept moving and succeeded in declining their hoisting efforts.

One older man grabbed his arm in a viselike grip and waved a program in his face. "You've got to sign this for my grandson, Hilton. He's a quarterback too! Hey, quit shoving for a minute. I've got to get this boy's autograph for my grandson. Best quarterback in the country!"

"WISH I COULD"

Chip eventually made it to the runway and the tunnel and the door of the locker room. There he was blocked again, this time by a crowd of fans of all ages who were jammed right up against the door. Inside, Chip could hear his teammates celebrating. Then he was recognized and besieged again. He finally fought his way through and pounded on the door. Murph Kelly cautiously inched the door open and pulled him inside.

"Well, well, look who finally made it!" he laughed.

Chip's previous encounters had been mild in comparison. He was greeted with a barrage that included wads of athletic tape, pads, socks, and jerseys. Chip was then carried and pushed and dragged to the shower and unceremoniously shoved under the water, uniform and all. Kelly thrust a towel in his hands when he came out. That movement gave Chip his first chance to ask the question that had been on his mind ever since Lansing had been carried from the field.

"How is Tims? Is he OK?"

His teammates grew silent and crowded around Kelly. "He has a concussion. The doctors can't tell how bad it is until they take some X-rays. He seemed all right. Coach was still with him when I left."

Few of the players who had taken part in that hectic last quarter had realized Ralston hadn't been on the sideline. The others had been so engrossed that they hadn't given it any thought. All were amazed.

"You mean he didn't even see us win?"

"Wow! He left the game and went to the hospital with Tims!"

"Man, that's one for the book! What a guy!"

"Who ran the team?"

"*Rockwell!* You ought to know! He put you in the game!"

"I didn't even realize that."

Murph Kelly's report dampened the celebrating in State's locker room. Tims Lansing was popular with everyone. Chip, Soapy, Whitty, and Fireball dressed quickly. Outside, they found much of the postgame celebration and confusion they had left on the field. Many of the happy motorists had joined the student celebration, honking their horns, flashing their headlights, and flying STATE UNIVERSITY pennants out their windows. Cars were facing in every direction, hopelessly snarled up. Some celebrating horns turned irritable, adding to the commotion.

Chip surveyed the parking lots and said cheerfully, "Come on, guys. Let's go. We'll get to Tenth and State before most of these cars get out of the lot."

"What's your hurry?" Whitty complained, matching Chip's long strides. "It's only five o'clock. We've got an hour before we start work."

"Chip's got business," Soapy explained. "Don't you remember the two-man teenage picket line? Hey, that was pretty witty, wasn't it, Whitty? Wonder if I can say that again? Two-age, teen— Oh, forget it."

"Actually," Chip spoke up, "I want to get a head start on the evening. I've got to call Leah Cahill about the job."

Soapy chimed in, "You mean the dynamic, double-team sentry should soon be a thing of the past?"

Chip's pace quickened. "Hopefully."

Tony and Bucky weren't in sight when they got to Grayson's, and Chip forgot all about them when the staff gathered around the four players.

"We heard it on the radio. Gee-Gee Gray got so excited when Chip made the field goal he couldn't talk!"

"What's the story on Lansing? Gonna be OK?"

Just then the throng of students and its accompanying pandemonium arrived at Main and Tenth. As the fans began to go their separate ways, many of the celebrants headed for Grayson's.

"Here they come!" Soapy shouted. "Prepare to be busy for the rest of the evening! Hope some of them have money left after the game for my tips. But first, a few quiet moments to change."

Chip headed for the privacy and quiet of the stockroom to call Leah as Soapy, Whitty, and Fireball went to the employee lounge area. Chip left a message with Leah's sister and then joined his teammates. He found them relaxed—weary but happy. They could hear loud, demanding voices outside.

"C'mon, Mr. Grayson! We know he's back there. Give us a break!"

"Trot 'em out, George. Trot out the heroes!"

"We won't leave 'til you produce Hilton. That's a promise!"

Soapy opened the door and peered out. "Look at that mob," he said. "They've got Mr. Grayson backed up against the soda fountain."

Finley joined Soapy at the door. "Looks as if we're in for it, Chip. Here comes Mr. Grayson."

"You mean Chip's in for it," Whitty corrected. "I'm happy right where I am. Besides, they want Chip."

"Me!" Chip remonstrated. "Why me?"

George Grayson opened the door, smiling and shaking his head apologetically. "Sorry, fellows. I can't do anything with them. Maybe you'd better come out for a second before they get too excited." He preceded the boys, and they reluctantly followed. The crowd immediately sent up a good-natured cheer.

"Hooray, Hilton! Speech!"

"Yeah, Soapy! Nice goin', Fireball! Way to go, Whitty!"

Chip refused to make a speech, but Soapy wasn't so modest. The happy-go-lucky redhead climbed up behind the fountain and grinningly obliged.

"You see," he began, "it was like this! Coming out for the second half, I grabbed Curly Ralston by the arm. You all know Curly, of course. He's the guy who's got the best seat in the stadium and never sits down. All the guys call him Coach, but he's just plain ol' Curly to me. We're pals! Ahem!

"Well, anyway, I grabbed my old pal by the arm and I said, 'Curly, you wanna win this game?' He looked at me kinda funny, and I said, 'Look, Curly, you ain't runnin' this team right. In the first place, you're lettin' Brandon make all the touchdowns. Every football coach knows ya can't win like that and . . .'"

Just then, Chip caught sight of Leah Cahill off to the side as the crowd was entertained by Soapy's silliness. Chip moved away from Whitty and Fireball and motioned for Leah to join him in the stockroom.

"Hi, Leah, I just called and left a message for you with your sister."

"Congratulations on the game, Chip. I wasn't there, but it sounds like it must have been exciting."

"Soapy will somehow make it sound like a Super Bowl victory. But let's talk about the job and how Mr. Grayson and I think you'll be able to help out."

"That's why I—I, uh, came to see you, Chip. I—I have to withdraw my name, if that's what it's called. Dad and I talked after our interview, and he said it sounded OK, but then I found out on Friday that I made the varsity soccer team. Dad was happy for me about soccer. He knows how much I wanted to make the squad—especially since I've never made a school team before."

Chip listened as Leah continued. "We talked about my use of time and priorities. School doesn't come easy for me, and I have to really study to get my Bs. After we talked, I decided I can't do justice to my school work, play soccer, help out at home, watch after my sister, and take the job. Dad said I might be able to handle a part-time job after soccer though."

"I understand. Congratulations on making the soccer team. Feels good, doesn't it?"

"Thanks." Leah smiled and nodded. "Dad said it was important and right that I should see you in person and let you know. But I still wish I could take the job. I was nervous and wasn't sure how to tell you I couldn't take the job."

"I'm glad you came in. Sounds like you have a pretty close family. That's important. Be sure you let us know how soccer's going. Come on, let's see if Soapy has finished his speech."

As Leah turned and waved, Chip saw two familiar figures on the edge of the crowd. Tony Carlara and Bucky Husta were watching Soapy, their faces sour with contempt.

Chip moved slowly behind the counter next to the fountain and out the side door. Then he walked briskly up Tenth to Main and in the front door. He was standing directly behind Tony and Bucky when Soapy finished his speech, and the crowd gave the popular comedian an appreciative cheer.

Tony turned away in disgust and saw Chip standing beside him. The startled boy's black eyes opened wide with surprise and then narrowed. Recovering his poise quickly, he looked at Husta and said, "Well, what d'ya know! The big football hero!"

Chip grinned. "Look, everyone calls me Chip," he said easily. "I want to talk to you. How about joining me for a shake and a burger?"

The boys began to back away, and Chip continued

quickly. "Not here! At that little restaurant right down the block on Tenth. What do you say?"

Tony looked at Bucky and shrugged his shoulders. "Why not?" he said. "What have we got to lose?"

Chip led the way out the door and down Tenth Street to Pete's Restaurant in the middle of the block. The silence was awkward, and he tried to make conversation. "I take it you're not into football."

"Kid stuff!" Tony said shortly.

Chip was known in the restaurant, and the cashier smiled and jerked his head toward the radio in the corner. "They're talking about you, Hilton. Ears burning?"

Chip smiled and shook his head. "No. Hope it's good though."

There were several customers seated at nearby tables, and they turned to look at Chip. "You Chip Hilton?" one demanded.

Chip nodded. "Yes, sir."

The tall man got up and extended his hand. "Put it there, young man. That was some game you played this afternoon. Heard it on the radio. Gee-Gee Gray says you're the greatest." He grinned and gestured toward Tony and Bucky. "These guys on the team?"

Chip smiled. "Not yet. Just friends."

Tony grunted and slouched down in one of the booths lining the wall opposite the counter. Bucky slid in beside him.

"Want the usual, Chip?" the owner called.

"Yes, Pete, thanks. Add two chocolate shakes too." He turned to his companions. "I'm having a hamburger. How about you guys?"

When Tony and Bucky declined, Chip again tried to get the conversation going. "Either of you still interested in the job?"

"WISH I COULD"

Tony answered for both. "Us? *Uh-uh!* We're not interested."

"You have any idea why no one else has tried to get the job?"

Tony grinned knowingly. "Maybe I have and maybe I haven't," he said mysteriously.

Pete brought the burger and shakes then, and Chip took advantage of the interruption to think it over. It was tough going, but he felt he was making progress. Tony was the dominant figure and knew all the answers. Bucky was Tony's yes man, but he was not to be underestimated. He was older, bigger, and appeared tougher than Tony.

Chip decided to try an indirect approach. "I've got a tough job up there, Tony, and I need help. The person I was going to hire can't do it. So I'd appreciate it a lot if you can help me out. You must know *somebody* who needs a job."

Tony looked surprised that someone had gotten by them and took his time answering, sipping his shake, and obviously thinking it over. Finally he looked Chip directly in the eye. "You're gonna have trouble getting someone, man. And if you get someone, he won't hang."

"Why?"

Tony shrugged. "Just because."

Chip was becoming impatient, but he controlled his tone and tried again. "Not even if *you* recommended him?"

That hit home. Tony's black eyes brightened, and his tightly held lips loosened a bit, showing sparkling white teeth. Chip waited, his pulse speeding up as he recognized the signs. Tony liked a pat on the back, but Chip could tell he wouldn't have admitted that fact for the world.

"What kind of kid do you want?" Tony demanded abruptly.

"Someone who needs help, Tony. I'd like to give the job to someone who helps out at home. Somebody who's reliable and isn't afraid to work."

Tony hooked a thumb at Bucky. "Not like us, huh?"

Chip grinned. "Frankly, no!"

Tony thought about that for a few seconds. Then he pushed Bucky out of the way and stood up. "I'll think about it," he said gravely, pulling several dollar bills out of his pocket and casually tossing them on the table. "C'mon, Bucky."

Chip stood up and reached for the bills. "Wait a minute. I want to ask you something. How did you know I was the one to see about the job?"

Tony smiled. "That's easy. The cashier said all the applicants had to see you. She said no one else would do."

Chip held out the bills to Tony. "Here's your money. It's my treat. I asked *you*."

Tony waved his hand in protest. "Leave it for the tip," he said, swaggering toward the door.

Chip left shortly afterward and hurried through Grayson's Tenth Street entrance. Soapy's sharp eyes spotted him as he dashed back to the stockroom. "Where have you been?" he demanded excitedly. "*Why* don't you tell me where you're going? Guess what! Ralston was in! He said he wanted to thank you and the rest of us for our part in pulling the game out of the fire. How about that? Said he knew we could do it and wished he could have been there. Said video just wasn't the same.

"Another thing! Tims is gonna be OK. Coach said he'll be all right in a couple of days. He suggested we drop in at the med center to see him tomorrow afternoon. He said Tims wanted especially to see you. Wonder what that's all about? Who knows? I gotta run! We're swamped! Never saw such a hungry crowd. See you later."

Chip was swamped too. He was kept busy until after ten o'clock. He had just sat down to write up some orders for supplies when there was a soft knock on the door. "Come in," he called.

There were two of them. The older boy was about fifteen and skinny. Chip judged that he weighed less than one hundred pounds. He had dark brown eyes and hair and an upturned nose. The other boy was a smaller version, but his weight was more proportional for his height. He had the same brown eyes and hair, but his nose was definitely buttonlike. Chip figured he was nine or ten years old. Both were dressed plainly, but their clothes were clean.

The older boy hesitated and then spoke in a low, half-fearful voice. "The lady at the cash register said to see you." The boy was shy and seemed able to speak only because of some special urgency.

Chip smiled. "About the job?"

"Yes, sir. I—"

"Is this your brother?"

"Yes, sir."

"It's pretty late for you two guys to be out, isn't it? Your mom know where you are?"

"Well, uh, Mom moved away. Aunt Edith knows where we are. She lives with us."

"Where's your father?"

The boy squirmed. "He's home, I guess."

"You mean you're allowed out this late?" Chip persisted.

"Yes, sir. No, sir. That is, I have to have a job, sir, and I, that is Mark and I, thought if I came tonight I might have a better chance." He thrust his hands into the pockets of his jeans. "I—I'm a good worker. I've had a paper route for five years. Mark has it now."

"Mark?"

"Yes, sir. My brother, here. He's Mark." The boy hesitated and then continued with more confidence. "Mark has been helping me with the papers for a long time. He knows the route better than I do. We decided I could help him with most of the deliveries and then get down here and take over this job."

"What's *your* name?"

"Isaiah, sir, Isaiah Redding."

"How did you find out about this job, Isaiah?"

The older boy hesitated. "Why, uh, most all the guys in our neighborhood know about it, sir."

"You can call me Chip, Isaiah. I'd like that better."

"Yes, sir, Chip."

"Do you have to help out at home, Isaiah?"

"Well, we have chores and things we do for Aunt Edith."

"That's good," Chip responded. "But I meant about money."

"Oh, well, Pop works, but he jokes sometimes 'bout runnin' out of money before runnin' out of month. We give Aunt Edith the money from the paper route since she buys food and stuff for the house with it."

That struck home. "All right, Isaiah," Chip said decisively. "I'll give you the job on a trial basis."

He handed Isaiah an application. "Have a seat here and fill it out." He turned to Mark. "Would you like a Soapy special?"

"A what?" Mark shook his head in wonder.

"Just follow me," Chip said with a laugh as he led Mark to the counter.

"WISH I COULD"

The crowd had thinned out, and Grayson's was getting ready to close for the evening. Chip glanced at the clock. Ten minutes to eleven. It was too late for these two to be out.

Soapy grinned when Chip asked for two extra large chocolate cones and told Soapy to put them on his account.

"You got it, Chipper. Did you hire both of them?"

"Wish I could," Chip said. "I really wish I could."

Ten minutes later Chip's new assistant and his little brother had finished their cones. Chip read through the application and then handed Isaiah the job description he had prepared. "This outlines your duties, Isaiah. Know it for your first day. Now, come on out and meet the rest of the Grayson's staff."

Chip introduced Isaiah and Mark to Mitzi Savrill, the cashier, owner George Grayson, and the fountain crew. "Pretty late for you guys to be out, isn't it?" Soapy asked.

Chip answered for the boys. "It sure is! Come on, Isaiah. We'll walk you home."

Isaiah's face flooded scarlet and a half-scared expression flashed across his face. "No, sir, please. We'd like to go home by ourselves, sir. If you don't mind, sir. We have to—"

"Have to?"

"Yes, sir. It's only a few blocks. I'll be here Monday, sir." Isaiah backed hastily away, pulling Mark by the arm. "I'll be here as soon as we finish with the papers, sir—I mean, Chip. Just like you said. Good night, and thanks, thanks a lot!"

CHAPTER 6

Soapy's Project

SOAPY SMITH had grown up in the same neighborhood, attended the same elementary school, and played on the same middle and high school teams with Chip Hilton, his best friend and personal hero. Soapy was a charter member of the Hilton Athletic Club (the Hilton A. C.), the group of boys that had grown up practicing football, baseball, and basketball in Chip Hilton's backyard. He was as much at ease in the Hilton home as in his own. Even Hoops, the Hilton cat, thought Soapy lived at 131 Beech Street because he ate there most of the time. Furthermore, the two friends were roommates in Jefferson Hall and shared their fortunes, good or bad. Their long friendship had enabled them to acquire an insight into each other's thoughts. That insight kicked in after the two Redding brothers departed.

When Chip told Fireball and Whitty that he was going on ahead on some personal business and would join them later at Pete's Restaurant, Soapy knew instantly what Chip had in mind. The jovial redhead got a few minutes head start, sauntered out of the store, and turned the corner. Chip caught up with him at the end of the first block.

"They're on the other side of the street," Soapy said. "Man, this is *some* neighborhood!"

"It sure is," Chip agreed, looking at the vacant, littered lots and boarded up windows with a scattering of small, neat houses surrounded by chain-link fences. "It's a neighborhood that's gone through some huge changes over the years. Now it seems some residents are trying to hold on while others have given up or moved out."

"You're right," Soapy agreed. "You ever see a darker street? I'd be afraid to walk down here by myself. Hey, the Redding kids have stopped. Look at that! Look at all the kids on that corner. There must be twenty of them. Where are their parents? Why don't they make those kids go home?"

"It's a mystery to me," Chip said. "Hold it. Let's stop here a minute."

Soapy grasped Chip by the arm. "Look, Chip, Isaiah is talking to that Tony—what's his name?"

"Carlara," Chip added.

"What's the name of the other one?"

"Bucky. Bucky Husta."

"Those kids ought to be home in bed," Soapy grumbled. "It's nearly twelve o'clock. Good thing for us there's no football curfew on Saturday nights! What are their parents thinking about leaving kids out this late at night?"

Chip was watching the group, hardly listening to Soapy. Isaiah was talking to Tony Carlara, and Chip figured he was explaining that he'd gotten the job. But why? "Come on," he said abruptly. "Let's go."

"OK. How come Isaiah is talking to that Tony guy, Chip?"

"I don't know, Soapy," Chip said slowly. "I don't get it."

"You think there's some connection between Isaiah and those two little hoods, Chip?"

"It sure looks like it. The only thing I can figure is that Tony and Bucky made sure Isaiah Redding got the job."

"How could they do that?"

"Easy. As long as someone as tough or tougher didn't come along and want the job."

"Sure, I get it! They played sentry and kept the other kids away. That's why they kept waiting outside the store all the time."

"I think so. But why? Why Isaiah Redding?"

"Got me. But you know something, Chip? I think Isaiah is OK."

Chip nodded in the darkness. "Yes, Soapy, he does seem all right. But somehow I can't figure Isaiah being the type who would be friends with a pair like Tony Carlara and Bucky Husta."

"Me either. I wonder what the connection is. Heck, Isaiah seems to me like the kind of a kid you wanted for the job."

"He is, Soapy. That is, if he told me the truth. But there's something else. You remember Louie Edwards and Red Fleming? Remember how they bullied every kid in the neighborhood until they made the mistake of picking on Biggie's brother?"

"Sure I remember! And I remember the time they tried to pick on you too. What's this got to do with Louie Edwards and Red Fleming?"

"Nothing. Nothing except that Tony Carlara and Bucky Husta seem to be the same kind of guys. Maybe I'm imagining things. Come on. Forget it."

SOAPY'S PROJECT

Fireball and Whitty were waiting in the restaurant. Fireball looked up from his scrambled eggs. "That was fast," he said. "Why all the mystery?"

"Checking up on Ralston's football spies and cameras," Soapy whispered, looking around mysteriously. "They probably don't know there's no curfew on Saturday night."

Chip didn't join in the conversation. He was trying to figure out why Isaiah Redding had been so secretive about his relationship with Tony Carlara and Bucky Husta. He was still thinking about it when he got back to Jeff and went to bed.

Soapy was on the prowl at seven o'clock Sunday morning, but he disturbed only his Valley Falls friends. He surprised them, too, when he seriously advised them they could sleep in after they read the paper. Then he presented each with a paper opened to the sports page. A three-column picture showed Chip Hilton kicking the winning field goal in the Brandon and State game.

Chip didn't like all the publicity and particularly Soapy's part in advertising it. He took a long walk alone and then went to church. Afterward, he joined his friends at Pete's on Tenth Street for lunch. Then the whole crowd walked up to the medical center to see Tims Lansing. Tims was sitting up in bed reading a paper when they were admitted to his room. He greeted them warmly.

"Nice going, guys," Tims said. "That was *some* comeback!" He winked toward Chip and poked a finger at the paper. "You're better looking than this," he said, grinning.

Other teammates dropped in from time to time, and when the nurse poked her head in the door and reminded the players crowding the room that visiting hours were over, Lansing asked Chip to wait a couple minutes.

"You guys mind if I speak to Chip alone?" he asked.

When the others had gone, Lansing motioned Chip to a chair. "I guess you're wondering what this all is about.

"Well, it's about you. You're a great football player, Chip. The best I ever saw. You can do everything. I guess you're going to think this is funny, coming from me, but I think you can be even better. What I'm trying to say is awkward because—well, I don't know you very well—"

Chip smiled and interrupted. "If it's about football and running a team on the field and pulling a game out of the fire," he said, grinning, "believe me, I'll listen, all right. You taught me a lot yesterday, Tims, whether you know it or not." Chip stopped Lansing when the veteran quarterback began to protest.

"Yes, you did, Tims. I watched you every second yesterday in that second half before you got hurt. I can call every play you used right now, every one of them. I made so many mistakes in that first half it was pitiful. I ran the legs off the running backs when it didn't count. Then when we got up where we needed the push, we were out of gas."

Lansing shook his head. "I wasn't going to criticize, Chip. I didn't mean that. You see, I know just what Ralston expects from his quarterbacks because I learned it the hard way. I thought maybe I could help you by going over some game situations and checking the proper plays. If we could get together an hour a day you'd have it down by Saturday. Would you like to do it?"

"Absolutely! You just set the time."

It was agreed that Chip would come to the medical center when he didn't have classes and before practice until Tims got out. Then they would make other arrangements.

Chip's friends were waiting for him in the lobby.

Upon his return, they walked slowly back to Jeff. Chip spent the rest of the afternoon and evening hitting the books.

Curly Ralston and his coaching staff got as much of a lift from the last-ditch victory over Brandon as the team did. A new spirit seemed to grip every player on the squad. It was obvious in the players' talk and in their new confidence in handling the ball and running the plays.

Chip spent every possible minute with Tims, and a strong friendship developed between them. Then Tims got his discharge with the understanding that he would not practice or play for a week. On Thursday, after practice and following a discussion of the Washington University scouting notes, Ralston had all the players see their specific position coaches and excused the squad with the exception of Chip, Buzz Burk, and Mike McGuire. Burk and McGuire had been used at quarterback all week, and Chip knew that Ralston was taking no chance on another injury that would leave him without a replacement. Chip mentally thanked Tims Lansing when Ralston began to shoot questions fast and furious at the three quarterbacks.

"When do you use trap plays, Hilton?"

"Only when opponents expect a big yardage play, Coach."

"Explain that!"

"Well, when the opponents expect you to try for small yardage, say up to four yards for a first down, they usually concentrate on their line defense and use more players on the line in one alignment or another to beat the trap. So they're better prepared on short-yardage plays, but not on long-yardage opportunities."

Ralston shot a quick glance at Burk and McGuire. "Got that?" he demanded. "Understand it?"

Burk and McGuire nodded, and Ralston grunted with approval. "All right, Hilton. Now, speaking of small yardage, when should you use a slow-developing play?"

"Never on the first down, Coach. And seldom on a small yardage situation unless it goes to the outside."

"Why is that?" Ralston asked.

"Hard-charging opponents can break through and drop the ballcarrier for a loss if there is much delay on a play."

"Now, Burk, suppose the opponents are not overly aggressive in their rushing. What kind of plays would be best?"

Burk had spent a lot of time studying the plays, but it was evident he was not used to the quick thinking that is a must with a quarterback. "Er . . . if their line is like a waiting line, Coach, then I guess the best plays would be through the line or around the ends. If they're waiting, it means they will have time to drop back for passes or meet the point of attack if we don't smash through their line."

Ralston hesitated. "Well, that's partly right. What do you say, McGuire?"

"I think all the plays should be straight, hard-smashing line slants, Coach."

Ralston nodded vigorously. "Right! Run 'em off the field when they start waiting or are back on their heels when they rush. Now, McGuire, what if the field is wet and the ball is slippery? What kind of plays would you use?"

McGuire hesitated. "I've heard you say a lot of times, Coach, that we shouldn't try to pass too much and that we ought to use simple plays and avoid double ballhandling as well as wide runs."

"That's right! Now, Hilton, on small yardage, assuming you want a first down, where is the best point of attack under our style of play?"

Chip could almost see Tims Lansing using that play against Brandon. Tims and he had discussed that very situation in the back of the library right after lunch. "To the short side, Coach. Inside the defensive left end or tackle."

Ralston grinned. "Had your eyes open in that third quarter on Saturday, didn't you? Good! Now, Hilton, while you're answering the questions, if you're in a tight spot and need a couple of yards for a mighty important first down, what would decide your choice of the play?"

"Two or three things, Coach. Our position on the field, the down, the alignment of their defense—"

Ralston waved a hand in protest. "I'm talking about the player to carry the ball as much as I am the play, Hilton."

"Yes, Coach. I'd use the back who had been doing the best running, and I'd call the play he'd been running most successfully."

That answer pleased Ralston, but it didn't stop the questions. He snapped them out and kept it up for the better part of an hour. "Good," he said finally. "Now, one last question. When is the best time to pass? You answer that, Hilton."

"I think the best time to pass is on small-yardage downs, Coach. Such as second down and three yards or less to go for a first down. Taking the time to play, the score, and the position on the field into consideration, naturally."

Ralston seemed satisfied. "Wait a second, men. This is the last. Now, Hilton, how do you camouflage your best deep pass?"

"It should be on a small-yardage down, sir. And it should look like an end run to the wide side of the field with a play action fake to freeze the defense. As an option, you could even have the fullback or one of the halfbacks throwing the ball after getting a pitchout. Finley is a good passer, Coach, and I think I would use him to throw the ball if I were calling the plays."

Ralston rose to his feet. "Thanks, men. We'll continue this some other time. You all had a good day's practice."

Chip was fifteen minutes late when he arrived at Grayson's, but Isaiah had everything under control. Isaiah hustled every minute. In fact, he was so devoted to his work that Chip didn't have the heart to ask about Carlara and Husta. So Chip decided to talk to Mark Redding. Mark often dropped by to help Isaiah, but Chip figured he was really interested in the banana splits and other goodies Soapy, Fireball, and Whitty bought for him. Chip did manage to get Mark to invite him to their home on Sunday afternoon.

Isaiah surprised Chip later that evening. He busied himself unnecessarily in the stockroom for a few minutes and then blurted out, "I wish I could be a football player."

"You can be," Chip assured him. "You just need to put on some weight and learn how to handle yourself on a football field. Come here. Let's see, how much you do weigh? Hmmm. Ninety-five pounds. That's not very much, is it? Let's see. We might as well start with posture and breathing. Turn around.

"Push your shoulders straight back. Good. Now, when I count, breathe in: one, two, three. Out: one, two, three. In: one, two, three. Get it? Now you practice those 'belly breaths' until I get back. Remember, shoulders straight *back,* not *up!*"

SOAPY'S PROJECT

Out at the fountain, Soapy listened enthusiastically as Chip told him about Isaiah. "You mean he can be my special project?" Soapy exclaimed. "Well, you just watch! Wait 'til I put him on the ol' Soapy Smith meal plan. I'll have him as plump as Tiny Tim McCarthy before Christmas. Wait and see! I'll start right now! Be back in a minute."

Chip went back to the stockroom, and Soapy appeared almost on his heels with a big container. "Isaiah, drink this!" Soapy said, ruffling Isaiah's hair. "You're gonna have three of these fruit shakes every night, compliments of your Grayson's coaching staff, Fireball Finley, Whitty Whittemore, and yours truly. OK?"

"Thanks, Soapy! Hey! Maybe I'll ask Aunt Edith to buy me some of that stuff that helps put on muscles, whatever it's called," Isaiah said, wiping banana milk shake from his mouth with his shirt sleeve.

In unison, Chip and Soapy yelled, "No!"

Soapy continued, "That stuff's not good for you! Nobody on our team uses that stuff—State's team doctor and trainers won't allow it. So your trainers aren't allowing it either. That's us. Got it?"

Chip added, "Isaiah, no one knows the long-term effects of those chemicals on the body, so stay clear of them. Soapy's fruit shakes are nutritionally good for you. They're just low-fat milk, fruit, and ice cream. Understand?"

The Grayson's crew didn't fool around after closing that night. The team was leaving at ten the next morning, and it was important that every player be home before the eleven-o'clock curfew.

There was a big crowd of student fans outside University Stadium on Friday morning as the team boarded buses for the drive to Washington University. The players got some fine cheers and some good advice.

"Make it win number three!"

"Stomp the Dukes!"

"Stay on top!"

After the buses pulled out of University for the four-hour ride, Chip settled down in his seat beside Soapy and prepared for a good snooze. He had just reached the pleasant, relaxed semistupor that precedes real sleep when Soapy dug an elbow viciously in his ribs. "Now what?" Chip growled, glaring at Soapy. "What's the matter with you?"

Soapy shifted his eyes upward, and then Chip saw Ralston standing in the aisle with Buzz Burk and Mike McGuire. He shot to his feet, wide awake. "Oh, Coach," he managed. "I . . . I was half asleep."

"So I noticed. That's all right, Hilton," Ralston said, smiling. "I thought it might be a good time for us to get together and talk a little strategy."

Soapy slid out in the aisle. "Well, I guess you won't be needing me," he said, clearing his throat. "Now if this was a little talk about stimulus—response conditioning, reinforcement theories, psychology lab experiments, or the science of banana split-ology . . ."

CHAPTER 7

Trash on the Corner

RALSTON STARTED right in as if there had been no interruption in the strategy quizzing of the preceding afternoon. He began with Chip and continued the passing discussion. "We talked about the best time to pass and the best way to conceal a long pass yesterday. Suppose we just continue in that vein. In what area on the field would you use a long, deep pass?"

"Usually anywhere between our own thirty-yard line and the opponent's thirty, Coach."

"Right. Burk, what should you do when your receivers are all covered and you are being rushed?"

Burk wasn't too sure of his answer, but he tried. "Lots of passers throw the ball away in that situation, Coach. They try to ground it. But I know you don't want us to do that, so I guess I'd try to run the ball."

Ralston turned to McGuire. "What would you do, McGuire?"

"I think I'd just take the loss, Coach, rather than make a wild throw or try to run wide and be thrown for a big loss or turn over the ball on a fumble."

"Good," Ralston agreed. "That's absolutely right. Intentionally grounding a pass is against the rules and against the spirit of the game. Besides, it's dangerous. You should drive straight ahead and try to keep from losing too much ground."

"What territory is usually open in any pass defense, Hilton?"

"The area in front of the safety man."

"That's right. It's the safest too."

Ralston continued the quiz for another half-hour and then moved on to another group. Chip took his nap and dozed until Soapy woke him again as the buses made their stop for lunch. Eating on the road and away from the usual college food was a treat for the college athletes.

The buses arrived at Washington University at three o'clock. Ralston and the Washington athletic department hosts led the squad to the visiting locker room. Then, instead of the full workout they had expected, Ralston surprised them. "No hard contact work today, men. Be dressed and on the practice field in thirty minutes. Be sure you're taped. We're going through our complete offensive and defensive series in preparation for tomorrow," he said.

Practice was still demanding as Ralston had his coaches put all the players, especially the quarterbacks, through their paces. After Ralston called the entire team to the center of the field for end-of-practice remarks, he singled out Chip to meet with the offensive and defensive coordinators. While his teammates, coaches, trainers, and managers headed to the locker room, Chip remained on the field with Ralston, Rockwell, and Sullivan.

TRASH ON THE CORNER

Chip wasn't expecting the news he received.

Only Curly Ralston spoke. "Chip, after thinking and then talking it over with our coaches here, I've decided you're the starting quarterback for tomorrow."

Chip was elated but sensed something else was coming.

Ralston continued. "Based on our depth charts, you're too valuable offensively, especially with Tims not here, to be in on some defensive plays. Until further notice, you'll focus on offense. At this stage, we'll still send you in on kickoffs, point-after-touchdowns, and field goals—in most cases. Maybe punts too. Understand?"

"Yes, Coach."

"Good, now relax this evening. You've got a busy day tomorrow."

Chip had mixed feelings about the news until the Rock winked and smiled that crooked smile in his direction as Ralston ended their meeting.

Soapy and the rest of the Hilton A. C.—Soapy, Red, Speed, and Biggie—were nearly dressed when Chip entered the locker room. "Hurry up, Chip! There's got to be food waiting for us somewhere, and then we're off to the movies."

Chip slept fitfully and awakened the next morning, lazily glad that State's game-day schedule called for the pregame meal at eleven o'clock. He remained in bed until ten o'clock and then ate lightly. And, once more, he was the first man dressed for the game. This time, Chip didn't fuss with his uniform. He sat, calm and collected, and planned his campaign for the afternoon. He had made up his mind to run the team according to Tims Lansing's book.

Ralston started Whittemore and Higgins at the ends, Cohen and Maxim in the tackle slots, McCarthy and

Smith at the guard positions, and Captain Mike Brennan at center. The starting backfield was Morris, Gibbons, Finley, and Hilton.

Mike Brennan won the toss and elected to receive. Several teammates cast quick glances toward Chip, who was standing on the sidelines, as Wynn Burnett took Chip's customary place near Fireball Finley as they readied to receive the kickoff. Chip glanced along the line of Washington University starters. They were well set and looked sharp. Then the kicker's toe plunked into the ball, and the game was on.

The kick was short and drove straight into Finley's arms. Fireball dug right up the middle to the State forty-five-yard line before he was buried under a mass of green-and-white-clad tacklers.

Chip remembered Tims Lansing and startled every player in the huddle when he called for a pass. It clicked! Whittemore was closely played by two Washington University defenders, but Chip pegged the ball to him anyway. All three went up for the ball, but two long red-and-blue-clad arms plucked the ball out of the air. Whitty held it as he tumbled down on the thirty.

Chip came right back with another success. He sent Fireball around right end, apparently on an end run. But Fireball stopped, planted his feet, and zipped the ball to Higgins in the end zone. State had scored in the first two minutes of play! The Washington University stands were silent, stunned by the suddenness of the score.

Washington University came back fighting. Chip kicked to the goal line, and Finley dropped the ball carrier on the twenty-yard line. Then the home players fought their way down the field in short, desperate line plunges that were determined and smooth. But their drive fizzled out before they could get into scoring territory, and State took the ball on its own thirty-five.

Chip immediately took over the offense and began driving downfield. State controlled the football for most of the first quarter, and Washington never got its game plan going as the clock moved into the second quarter.

Then Washington managed to hold the Statesmen to three downs. As Chip punted, the Washington University punt return man was surrounded by State tacklers and signaled for a fair catch. Washington began pounding the line all over again, using the antiquated formula of "hit the line on first down, run the ends next, pass on third down, and kick on the fourth."

On the sidelines, Chip shook his head. If it hadn't been for Tims Lansing's tutoring sessions, the tactics employed by the Washington University quarterback might well have been Chip's own. It was bad football, and it showed up in the score. State had an easy time and led 21-0 at the half.

In the second half, Ralston eased up and cleared his bench. The State replacements clicked for another touchdown, and Ralston sent Chip in long enough to kick the extra point. Washington University managed to score in the last quarter, and Chip booted a thirty-yard placement seconds before the end of the game. The final score: State 31, Washington University 6.

Somehow, Chip didn't feel very good about the game. The contingent of State supporters in the visitors' section celebrated the victory as a great feat, but Chip and his teammates knew the score could just as easily have been 60-6. Ralston just didn't believe in humiliating an opponent.

The State squad left the Washington University campus at six o'clock, but it was nearly midnight before the happy players could relax and get back to their dorms and in bed.

From a deep sleep, Chip heard pounding on doors, but it wasn't until his roommate shoved him roughly and pushed a copy of the *Herald* under his nose that he was almost awake.

"Look!" Soapy said excitedly. "Another picture! And read what Bill Bell has to say in his column. It's great!"

Chip sat up slowly and stared at the picture. It had been taken in the first game of the season and showed him executing his part of the play that resulted in Philip Whittemore's winning touchdown against Tech. "Not again," he muttered. "This is no good."

"Oh, yes, it is," Soapy corrected. "Read Bill Bell's column."

"You don't understand, Soapy," Chip said, shaking his head. "This isn't fair to the rest of the team. What's Bill Bell trying to do?"

"I guess he knows what he's doing," Soapy said complacently. "He's been writing sports for forty years."

"I don't mean that."

"C'mon, Chip. Remember what I told you when we were sitting on the bench in the Brandon game. You play like Chip Hilton ought to play all the time and let the blocks fall where they may. You hear?"

Chip read the caption under the picture.

> *William "Chip" Hilton, State quarterback, setting up the winning play in the thrilling first game against Tech.*

Then he shifted over to Bill Bell's column.

TRASH ON THE CORNER

STATE ROLLS OVER
WASHINGTON UNIVERSITY, 31-6
by Bill Bell

State's powerful, quick-striking team made it three in a row here this afternoon. Much of the credit for the easy victory goes to Curly Ralston's sophomore quarterback sensation, who called his plays perfectly.

Hilton's opening-play pass struck with devastating speed, and the second aerial, fired by Finley to Higgins, was good for a touchdown before half of the fans in the Washington University stadium realized the game was underway. Hilton then kicked the extra point, and State led 7-0 before the game was two minutes old.

Overmatched Washington University made a gallant fight when it had the ball, but State had too much strength for the hometown forces. State won its third game of the season, 31-6, before 43,184 spectators.

Last year, you may remember, I identified an unknown player in the university dorm league as the greatest varsity prospect I'd ever seen. The player, Chip Hilton, pictured elsewhere on this page, quarterbacked Jeff into the dorm championship and later represented State in the freshman game against the A & M yearlings on Thanksgiving day.

Yes, it's the same youngster, the leader of Jeff's Cinderella Kids.

Here's an excerpt from that story: "This year's championship team, Jefferson, proves something else—proves kids can work and study and still play an outstanding game. Seven of the eleven starters are working while attending college. And every player on the starting team passed his midterm exams with an average of 80 percent or better."

Now back to the present: *Four* of the players who started for Curly Ralston against Washington yesterday were members of that Cinderella team—and six of the Cinderella Kids are on the squad.

"What's wrong with that?" Soapy demanded, grinning happily.

Chip smiled. "I'll bet you passed these all over the dorm," he said reproachfully, beginning to dress. "It's embarrassing."

Soapy was demoralized. "But why, Chip? Why?"

"It isn't false modesty, Soapy. I like to see my name in the sports page just like anyone else, and I'm proud to be on a State team. It's just that the attention makes me feel funny. It's embarrassing, that's all."

Chip soon found out he didn't have to worry about his teammates. They were as proud of the sports article about him and his friends as they had been of his success on the field. They added their congratulations to Soapy's.

"Man, I'd give my right arm if Bill Bell would write a column like that about me!"

"Let's hope he keeps writing 'em all season!"

"He will! We've got it made! A & M, here we come!"

Chip went to church and had lunch with the Jeff crew. Then he started out to visit Isaiah Redding and his family. He walked down Main Street, turned the corner, and walked past Pete's Restaurant. It was closed, so he continued down Tenth Street four blocks until he saw the pizza place on the corner. A block away he recognized Tony Carlara and Bucky Husta hanging out on the corner talking to several others. As Chip approached, he felt the antagonism in the battery of eyes that looked him over.

TRASH ON THE CORNER

It was obvious which one was the leader. Chip didn't have to be told. "Hello, Tony," he said. "Can you tell me where Isaiah Redding lives?"

Tony took plenty of time answering, measuring Chip up and down as he had that first time, apparently more for effect than for any other reason. "Sure," he drawled insolently, staring boldly at Chip. "Why you wanna know?"

Chip smiled, trying to conceal his irritation. "Because Isaiah invited me to his house," he said patiently.

There was a long, heavy silence, and Chip could feel the wall of dislike, almost hate, that seemed to spring up between the group and himself. *What's wrong with these kids?* he asked himself.

Tony studied Chip a long minute and then hooked a thumb contemptuously over his shoulder. "Fourth house on the left," he said shortly, turning back to his companions.

Chip hesitated and then walked slowly away, half angry and half hurt by the treatment. He normally made friends easily. But this reception only added to his resolve to uncover the mystery of Isaiah's association with Tony Carlara and Bucky Husta.

The Reddings rented a narrow, two-story faded brick house. The two adjacent houses had been painted years earlier, as evidenced by the red brick showing through. Chip noticed each had worn wooden porches leading to doorways. He paused as he looked up and down the street, surveying the empty lots and small houses and larger buildings he'd only seen after dark. He walked up the four steps onto the porch and immediately noticed that the doorbell wires had been pulled out several inches, as if left undone and in some stage of repair. He lifted his hand to knock, but before he could tap on the glass, the door flew open.

Mark greeted Chip with his slow smile. "Hi, Chips! Come on in! We've been expectin' you."

Chip followed Mark into the house and down a narrow hallway. Chip noticed the well-worn, once-green runner. On the left was a small, sparsely furnished living room. As they passed the stairs, he took a glimpse at the loosened handrail. Mark delivered him into the dining room. It seemed to Chip that the whole family was gathered in the room. A middle-aged woman was hastily clearing dishes off a table. Isaiah leaped from a chair where he had been reading a newspaper. Chip saw that it was the *Herald* and that it was opened to the sports page containing his picture.

"Man, Chip, congratulations! This is some write-up! Oh, I want you to meet my family. This is our Aunt Edith."

Chip shook hands with the tired-looking lady who smiled gently.

"I'm glad to meet you, Mr. Hilton," she said softly. "I'm Edith Clark. I feel as though I know you." She gestured toward Isaiah and Mark. "The boys talk about you so much. Won't you sit down?"

"Thank you, Mrs. Clark. But, please, everybody calls me Chip."

Chip sat down and then met Della, Tara, Beth, and Tammy, who were all younger than Mark. "That's the family," Isaiah said proudly. "All except Pop. He's asleep. I'll call him."

Chip stopped him. "No, that's OK, Isaiah. I'll meet him some other time." It seemed to Chip that Isaiah's face registered relief.

It was a pleasant visit. Chip enjoyed talking with the

little girls, and Isaiah's aunt had a warm personality and a good sense of humor. Although the surroundings were eloquent evidence of the family's financial situation, Chip heard only happiness and love in his hour's stay. Chip was sincere when he said good-bye and promised to come again, soon. Isaiah and Mark accompanied him from the dining room. Just as they reached the end of the hall, a door on the left opened, and a man thrust his head out.

"Where you going, Isaiah, Mark?" the man demanded sharply. Then, seeing Chip, he paused uncertainly.

"This is Mr. Hilton, Pop," Isaiah explained. "The man I work for—"

Mr. Redding extended his callused hand. "Glad to meet you, Hilton," he said abruptly. He hesitated a second and then stepped back in the room. "Now don't you kids go near that trash on the corner," he said sharply. "You hear, Isaiah? You hear, Mark?"

CHAPTER 8

An Overdose of Meanness

TONY CARLARA and his corner cadre were still hanging out in front of the pizza place when Chip passed. But their averted glances and sudden concentration on something in the other direction made it clear they didn't want to speak. Chip continued, thinking about Isaiah. He was completely sold on his assistant and the whole Redding family. What he had learned that afternoon about Isaiah's responsibilities was enough for Chip. His brisk pace soon brought him to Jeff, where he spent the rest of the day studying.

Football was the main topic of conversation on the campus Monday morning, and Chip was the center of interest in his classes. He sighed with relief when his third class ended and he could meet Tims Lansing for lunch. Waiting outside the student union, Tims welcomed Chip with a big smile.

"Congratulations, Chip. Nice going! I read the story of the game in the Sunday papers. It was terrific! I liked that first pass."

AN OVERDOSE OF MEANNESS

"Thanks to you," Chip said. "I'd never have called that pass if it wasn't for you."

Lansing grinned. "I couldn't help you now, Chip. You're a postgraduate."

"Well, I don't feel like one!" Chip protested. "I need your help now more than ever. If you can take time off from your own football."

"I'm afraid there isn't going to be anymore football for me, Chip. Dr. Terring sidelined me for another three weeks. The season will be over before I can get back in shape. My football-playing days are over."

"No!"

Lansing nodded grimly. "That's what the man said. Come on, let's eat. I'm starved."

They joined the cafeteria line and carried their trays to an unoccupied table in a corner. After they finished eating, Lansing pulled the morning paper out of his pocket and handed it to Chip. "Read what Jim Locke has to say about our chances for the conference title."

A & M LOOMS AS CONTENDER FOR NATIONAL HONORS
Conference Champions Win Number 12
by Jim Locke

Powerful, all-victorious A & M took another step this Saturday toward a national title by racking up victory number twelve over Brandon University by a score of 33-6. The Aggies have won five straight this year, running wild over Wesleyan, Washington, Tech, and Brandon, and outscoring Southwestern 30-13. A & M has scored 170 points to their opponents' 21 this season, and the all-veteran team seems stronger than ever.

FOURTH DOWN SHOWDOWN

> Local fans, unreasonably enthusiastic because of State's three-game winning streak, are beginning to compare the locals with A & M. A comparison of scores quickly shatters the illusion. State defeated Tech by a last-second touchdown; A & M defeated the Engineers 28-2. State barely squeaked by Brandon 17-14; A & M swamped the same team 33-6. State beat Washington 31-6; A & M buried the Washington forces 51-0. Enough said.

Lansing chuckled when Chip finished reading the article. "Really likes us, doesn't he?"

"Guess he likes A & M more," Chip replied. "Can't blame him for that."

"Time will tell," Lansing said grimly. "I've already talked to Coach Ralston about not being able to play anymore, and I also said I wanted to help with the quarterbacks for the rest of the season. So how about a little football quarterbacking?"

"Absolutely! I put in six hours of studying time yesterday, and I'm through until practice. Let's go."

Chip spent two hours with Lansing at their favorite library table and then headed for practice. Because his muscles were stiff from the Washington game, he was eager to get out on the field and loosen up. Upon hurrying into the locker room, he was surprised to find it deserted except for the trainer. Chip stopped and looked around. "Where is everybody, Murph? No practice today?"

"Oh, there's practice, all right. Up in the meeting room. Coach is getting soft. Says you players need a rest. This modern game beats me. When I was a young man, we played our football on the field. Now it seems about all the coaches want to do is run film and draw funny little diagrams on a board. It's something!"

AN OVERDOSE OF MEANNESS

Ralston's meeting-room procedure was old stuff to State's varsity. The famous coach believed that more football games were won with brains than brawn. Soapy and Biggie were saving a chair for Chip, and he sat between them. At 3:45 sharp Rockwell rapped on his chair, and Ralston moved to the board.

"Men," he began, "we're going to cut this practice short. But before we let you go, we want to tell you about our plans for Saturday. Southwestern is our next opponent, and they're good.

"I'm sure you know their record as well as I do, but it's wise to keep in mind that they won the Sugar Bowl last year and have an all-veteran team. They've lost only to A & M. Coach Sullivan scouted them Saturday and thinks they will predominately use a five-man defensive line because"—Ralston paused and chuckled—"because we have discovered the value of the pass as a part of our offense. They will work to shut it down with their five-man front or by showing four on the line and rushing one or more of their linebackers.

"Now I'm *not* going to put all our pass plays on the board to check the blocking against a five-man line, but I am going to discuss a couple of plays so we'll know what to expect." Ralston quickly drew the play on the board.

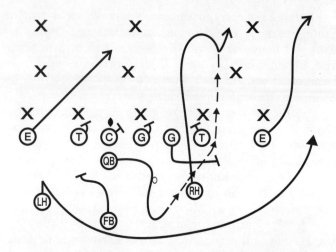

Even a football novice would have appreciated Ralston's skill at drawing plays. After drawing the play, he tapped the board with the marker and continued: "The quarterback first fakes a handoff to the right halfback, who drives straight ahead. The second fake is to the left halfback cutting behind the quarterback and around the right end. Good faking by the backs on this play is vital. The right halfback turns on the count of ten for the pass. Any questions?"

Ace Gibbons cleared his throat and raised his hand. "Coach," he said hesitantly, "the linebacker hit me Saturday almost as soon as I caught the ball. Washington used a six-man defensive line, but I was wondering if our right end couldn't cut to the outside of their other linebacker on that side and get downfield a little faster. Seems I was in the secondary before he was."

Ralston nodded. "I noticed that, too, Ace. It's a matter of timing and how well the defense has blocked. You'll have to delay at the line a little longer and our right end will have to get away faster. Are there any other questions on this play? No? Good. Now the buttonhook to the left halfback."

Ralston continued talking as he drew the second play on the board. "I guess you've gathered by this time that we intend to do a lot of passing. Exactly what Southwestern expects. And we think the buttonhook series is the most effective type of pass we can use against a 5-3-3 defense. So we want you to think about these until tomorrow afternoon. Now, let's take a good look at the buttonhook to the left halfback.

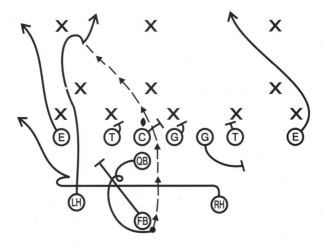

"Now this buttonhook to the left halfback is a take-off on our fullback smash to the weak side. The faking by the backs is even more important than it is on the buttonhook to the right back. The right halfback is in motion to the left on the count of two. The quarterback first fakes to him, then to the fullback, and then cuts back to the passing slot, concealing the ball.

"The halfback and the fullback must pull good fakes and hold them for a count of eight. The ends must sprint directly toward the defensive backs and then buttonhook left or right, according to the signal. Any questions?" There was a short silence. Ralston continued, "All right then, let's keep thinking about Southwestern's 5-3-3 defense. That's all."

Soapy followed Chip out through the players' gate, trying to keep in step with Chip's long strides. "What's the rush?" he complained.

"Incoming deliveries! A million of them! It's the same every Monday."

Chip was surprised to find the stockroom door locked. He checked with Mitzi and learned that Isaiah had not arrived for work. The stockroom phone rang at 6:30; it turned out to be his assistant. Isaiah's voice was tense and anxious.

"Chip, this is Isaiah. I'm awful sorry, but I'm sick. I guess I can't come to work."

"What's wrong, Isaiah?"

"I'm just sick. Mark said he would tell you after he finished delivering the papers, but I didn't want you to worry."

"Where are you calling from, Isaiah?"

"The pizza shop. Our phone isn't working."

"Did you see the doctor?"

"No, sir. I'll be all right in a couple of days, I think."

"All right, Isaiah. You hurry home and stop worrying. You better get right to bed. Good night."

As Chip cradled the receiver, he thought it over. Isaiah sounded awful, but something about the conversation puzzled him. Maybe Mark could be a little more specific.

AN OVERDOSE OF MEANNESS

Mark arrived about seven o'clock and managed to attract Soapy's attention on his way back to the stockroom. But Chip learned nothing from the little Redding. Mark clammed up completely when Chip tried to find out what was wrong with Isaiah. He disappeared immediately after downing the banana split Soapy made him.

Chip couldn't get Isaiah out of his mind. By 10:30, he was so concerned that he got permission from George Grayson to leave early. He knew he would have to hurry, but he was determined to find out what was really wrong with Isaiah.

The same crowd was hanging out on the corner. However, this time Chip kept going. He nodded in the direction of Tony Carlara, but he didn't care whether Tony acknowledged him. Chip could feel the unfriendly eyes boring into his back, and it was all he could do to restrain his impulse to spin around and challenge their arrogance. He was glad when he reached the brick house where Isaiah lived.

Isaiah's aunt opened the door. "Oh, Chip," she said, "come in. I suppose you came to see Isaiah. It's awfully nice of you; but he's in bed, and I'm afraid he's asleep."

"That's all right, Mrs. Clark," Chip said, stepping inside. "I'm in a hurry to get to the dorm and I can't stay, but I thought I'd drop by and see how he was feeling."

Mrs. Clark smiled. "Isaiah isn't feeling so bad physically, Chip. But his spirits are pretty low. You see, he's completely wrapped up in his job with you at Grayson's, and, well, frankly, I think that's what caused the trouble."

"Trouble?"

"Argument is probably the correct word. Anyway, Isaiah had some sort of an argument or scuffle with one of those boys down on the corner, and I guess he got the worst of it."

"You mean he was in a fight?"

"Well, it certainly looks like it. His face is scratched and he has a cut lip. I think he's going to have a black eye in the morning."

"Do you know who the fight was with?"

"He wouldn't talk about it, but one of the girls said the boy was older and bigger. She said Mark tried to help Isaiah, but some of the other boys held him and he couldn't do anything."

"When did this happen, Mrs. Clark?"

"Right after school. I've tried to keep the boys away from that crowd on the corner, but it's almost impossible. Isaiah and Mark work after school, of course, and what little spare time they have is usually spent at that dining room table with their books. But those other boys are *always* on that corner. And they *always* seem to be in some kind of trouble or causing it."

"Are you sure they didn't give any hint about whom Isaiah was fighting with, Mrs. Clark?"

"Well, the boys wouldn't tell me anything. But I overheard them talking in their room, and from what I could gather, his name is Bucky something."

Chip nodded. "Well, I'll have to get going, Mrs. Clark. Tell Isaiah to get well and not to worry about the job."

Chip paused on the sidewalk and thought it over. Now he knew. He looked at his watch. Ten minutes to eleven! Ten minutes to make it to Jeff and beat Ralston's curfew. It was going to be close.

Instead of going back to the pizza shop corner and turning up Tenth Street, Chip decided to take a shortcut and avoid Main Street. He turned left from the battered brick house and set out at a good, steady pace. The neighborhood got worse; the houses were more decrepit, and the lights seemed dimmer and farther apart. He

lengthened his stride. Then he heard the running footsteps, almost in time with his own. But he dismissed the
thought. The sound was probably the echo of his own
footsteps.

In a few minutes he'd left the rundown area behind
and entered a neighborhood of small, newer houses.
There were more people out walking here, and up ahead
he could see the stadium tower. He slowed down and
looked at his watch again. Three minutes! Then he heard
the running footsteps once more.

Directly ahead, the sidewalk was lined with large
trees. Just as the shadows darkened, Chip ducked
behind the trunk of one of the largest of the trees. The
runner was closer now, and Chip peered around the other
side of the tree. It was Soapy! Chip stepped out and
caught him around the body in a half-tackle. "Gotcha!
What's the idea?" he demanded. "Following me, huh?"

"What d'ya mean?" Soapy blustered. Then he capitu-
lated. "All right, so I was following you! You weren't fool-
ing me when you said you'd see me later and slipped out
the side door. Mr. Grayson let me off too. I knew where
you were going, and the rest was easy. How's Isaiah?"

Soapy listened restlessly as Chip repeated his conversation with Mrs. Clark. When Bucky Husta was mentioned, Soapy burned with anger. "I saw the little rat on
the corner," Soapy said with disgust. "He's twice as big as
Isaiah! Somehow that rat's got an overdose of meanness
and a barrel of poor sportsmanship."

CHAPTER 9

A Small Price to Pay

HENRY ROCKWELL was a player's coach: experienced, thorough, persistent, and patient. He was also Curly Ralston's chief assistant and offensive coordinator. He was responsible for the split-second timing required in the performance of Ralston's clever, often unbalanced plays. Rockwell had coached Chip in high school as an end for two years and then for two more as the Valley Falls High School varsity quarterback. Chip's wizardry with the ball was the result of hours of Rockwell's patient instruction while Chip was playing in high school. Rockwell never made personal references in his criticism; there was never a hint of anger, no heated tones, no ridicule, and no sarcasm when a mistake was made.

State's players enjoyed working with the veteran coach but not only because of his attitude. Rockwell was an expert at objectively analyzing a mistake. And then, he always had the patience to explain, in minute detail, the proper technique.

A SMALL PRICE TO PAY

It was apparent that State's coaching staff was concerned about Southwestern. Victory meant a long step toward conference leadership. Rockwell was sending the backs and ends through Ralston's intricate plays time and again. There was little Rockwell could teach Chip about handling the pigskin. Chip was uncanny in his ability to conceal the ball, fake handoffs to speeding backs, or find the open receiver for a pass. The veteran assistant coach had taught his protégé the proper techniques, but Chip was the only player Rockwell had ever known who could execute the correct moves and add something to them.

Tims Lansing, standing on the sidelines, concentrated on every movement Chip made. "He's the greatest!" he said aloud.

"Who's the greatest?" a nearby manager echoed.

"Chip. Chip Hilton. That's why he's the first-string quarterback."

"Tims, you're saying that just because you're a good sport. If you hadn't gotten hurt, you would've been the regular quarterback and you know it!"

Lansing shook his head. "Never in a million years. Believe me! I mean it! Watch this!"

Chip took the ball from Brennan, pivoted to the right, and with his left hand seemed to give the ball to Ace Gibbons racing through the right side of the line. Then Chip straightened up, watched Gibbons's progress, and with his right hand behind his back, apparently fed the ball to Fireball Finley cutting to the weak side. Moving lazily back, Chip watched the two ballcarriers as they sped in different directions.

"Fullback has the ball," the manager said confidently.

"*Maybe,*" Lansing said dryly.

At that moment Chip's indolent posture disappeared,

and his right arm streaked back and up. The ball whirled straight as a rope fifty yards upfield. Big Philip Whittemore gathered the spinning projectile on his fingertips without breaking stride.

There was a gasp of surprise from the manager. "I could have sworn the fullback had the ball! I thought Fireball had it. Hilton's a magician!"

"See what I mean?" Lansing drawled.

Rockwell worked through all the pass series, alternating each with a takeoff running play, and Chip threw passes until he thought his arm would fall off. Rock wasn't satisfied. Gibbons's fake wasn't quick enough, Finley faked too fast, and Morris's fake didn't fool anyone. Then the ends caught it. Whittemore buttonhooked left when he should have turned right. Higgins didn't start fast enough, Schwartz let the tackle slow him down, and Curtis gave away the direction he was going to cut by turning his head too soon.

When Burk and McGuire took turns at the quarterback position, nothing clicked. Rockwell's patience with the two players was unbelievable. Time after time he repeated a play, his clear, modulated voice showing no annoyance, no matter how serious the mistake. It was a long, monotonous, heartbreaking drill.

Ralston worked with the line in much the same fashion, calling the plays and checking the single- and double-team blocking—the timing, the charge, the high and low, the turn, the cross-body, the straight shoulder, the reverse body, the reverse shoulder, the standing block, and all the others that were part of the repertoire of a Ralston lineman.

Chip wasn't the only player who breathed a deep sigh of relief when Ralston bellowed, "That's all! Three and in!"

A SMALL PRICE TO PAY

A good shower and the brisk use of a towel did a lot for tired muscles. Chip was dead tired when he took off his football uniform, but he was full of energy when he put on his clothes. The jog with Soapy, Fireball, and Whitty down to Grayson's gradually eased his tight muscles.

On the way, half-listening to his friends' chatter, Chip caught himself thinking about his conversation with Isaiah's aunt. He hadn't thought much about it at the time, but later, one remark in particular had struck home. He could almost hear her now. "Isaiah is completely wrapped up in his job with you at Grayson's, and, frankly, I think that's what caused the trouble."

Mark Redding appeared in the stockroom at seven o'clock and reported that Isaiah was better. "Isaiah's black . . . er . . . I mean, Isaiah will be back tomorrow, Chip. I guess I'd better take over for him tonight. What do you want me to do first?"

Chip wanted to laugh, but Mark's serious expression stopped him. "Sorry, Mark. As much as I could use your help, Mr. Grayson and all of us would get into trouble if we let you work. Maybe in a few years."

"Aw, my age and a work permit don't make any difference, Chip. I deliver papers, don't I?"

"Maybe it's different with a paper route, Mark. Or maybe they think it's still Isaiah's route. Now listen. Do you want to do me a big favor?"

"Sure, Chip. Anything!"

"Well, I want to know about the fight. Why did Bucky Husta jump on Isaiah?"

Mark's brown eyes opened wide. "How'd you know it was Bucky?"

"I knew."

Mark's jaw squared, and his eyes narrowed. "I'm gonna beat him up real good just as soon as I'm a little bigger. He's nothin' but a bully. Isaiah might have got hurt bad if Mr. Caruso hadn't stopped it. Bucky never starts anything when Tony's around. Tony's tough, but he fights fair. That's more than you can say about Bucky! He's afraid of Tony."

"What was the fight about?"

Mark hesitated. "It . . . it was about you, Chip. Isaiah had the article from the paper—the one with your picture. He was showing it to the guys on the corner and telling them about you. Bucky must've got jealous and told him to shut up."

"Then what happened?"

"Well, Bucky said he didn't want to hear anymore about college dorks who just played wimpy games with lots of padding and couldn't fight or do something real. Then he told Isaiah something else, and, well, I can't tell you what that was about, and then they had a fight. Then Bucky pulled the article out of Isaiah's pocket and tore it up right in front of everybody. The man in the pizza place—that's Mr. Caruso—broke it up, but Isaiah got the worst of it, all right."

"I'm sure he did," Chip said. "What can't you tell me, Mark?"

"Well, you see—" A sudden look of fear crossed Mark's face, and he slowly shook his head. "I can't tell you anymore, Chip. You won't tell Isaiah I told you about the fight, will you, Chip?"

Chip shook his head. "I won't tell, Mark. Word of honor. Now let's go see Soapy and have some ice cream. Then you'd better go home. Right?"

Later, on the way to Jeff, Chip told Soapy, Whitty, and Fireball what he had learned about Isaiah's trouble. Whitty and Fireball were indignant, but Soapy was furious. It was all the others could do to keep him from going back right then to do something about Bucky Husta.

"Dirty rat!" Soapy fumed. "Jumping on a nice little guy like Isaiah. What for? Why would Husta want to beat *him* up?"

"I don't believe you got the whole story, Chip," Whittemore observed. "There's something else. Got to be!"

"Sure there is," Fireball agreed.

"Whatever it is," Chip said quietly, "I intend to find out. I think we'll have to be careful not to get Tony and Bucky and the corner crowd completely down on Isaiah. We'd better go slow about trying to help Isaiah too. I've only known him a short time, but I think the little guy would like to fight his own battles. Most kids do."

"I'd like to fight just one of his battles," Soapy replied. "Just one!"

"It's a shame someone can't do something about that bunch," Chip mused aloud. "It's not right for those kids to be hanging around on that corner at all hours of the day and night."

"No one could do anything with that bunch, Chip," Soapy said hotly.

"We'll see," Chip said softly.

Everyone was silent the rest of the way home. Each went to bed wishing he could fight Isaiah Redding's battles.

If he had known the extent of the affection and loyalty his new friends felt toward Mark and himself, Isaiah would have figured a black eye, a cut lip, and a few bruises to his body and pride were a small price to pay indeed.

CHAPTER 10

Now It's Up to the Kids

GEORGE GRAYSON was overseeing a new window display Wednesday evening when Isaiah arrived for work. The owner's keen eyes took in Isaiah's swollen face and multicolored eye, but he said nothing. Later, however, he called Chip to his office. "What happened to your new assistant?" he asked directly.

Chip told Mr. Grayson about Isaiah's trouble with Bucky Husta and described the interest Soapy, Fireball, and Whitty had taken in the boy. George Grayson smiled broadly when Chip told him about Soapy's efforts to put some bulk on the youngster's skinny frame.

"I agree with Soapy," he said, nodding his head. "Someone should beef him up. Tell Soapy I'll chip in on the cost of those shakes." He reflected a moment and then continued. "Tell you what, I'll pay for all the shakes if Soapy and his fountain crew will donate Isaiah a membership in the YMCA. All right?"

Chip told Mr. Grayson that it was more than all right

and hurried downstairs to tell Soapy the good news. Then they began to work in earnest with their protégé. Soapy practically floated Isaiah in fruit shakes, and the youngster began to gain weight. When the redhead got Isaiah on the scales Friday evening, Isaiah weighed an even ninety-eight pounds.

"It's a new record," Soapy boasted. "Now for one hundred!"

Chip stuck to his program. He encouraged Isaiah with his studies and utilized every opportunity to teach him something about boxing and wrestling. After Soapy had weighed Isaiah the following Friday night, Chip grasped his assistant by the arm, ushered him out the front door, and hurried him up Main Street.

"Where we going?" Isaiah demanded, lengthening his stride and trying to match Chip's pace.

"We're going to the Y," Chip said firmly. "Mr. Grayson's on the board of directors, and he wants me to sign you up for a junior membership."

Isaiah stopped abruptly. "No way," he said, pulling back. "I'm not joining any Y."

"But you want to learn boxing and tae kwon do, don't you?"

"Yes, but I'm not joining any Y to learn boxing or tie condos—whatever that is."

"Sure, why not?" Chip asked. "Come on, it's only going to take a minute, and it won't hurt."

"But I can't afford it!" Isaiah persisted. "I've got to work."

"It's all paid for," Chip assured him. "Soapy, Fireball, and Whitty chipped in for the membership fee, and Mr. Grayson said you could have an hour off every night to attend the classes. OK?"

"But none of the guys around my neighborhood belong to the Y, Chip. It means trouble for me."

"Trouble!" Chip echoed. "What do you mean?"

Isaiah shook his head, looked at the ground, and pressed his lips into a thin line. "Nothing, never mind," he said in a low voice.

Signing up took only a few minutes, and then they were ushered to the big gymnasium. There were two instructors on the floor, each surrounded by a small group of boys. One instructor was teaching boxing in a regular ring set in the middle of the gym, and the other was demonstrating tae kwon do forms. Isaiah's eyes lit up, and he moved purposefully toward the tae kwon do class. Chip followed, jubilant because of Isaiah's apparent interest. Fifteen minutes later he was hustling back to Grayson's, highly pleased with himself.

"How'd things go?" Soapy asked.

Chip paused at the fountain. "You should have seen him," Chip said, grinning. "Pitched right in! The last thing I saw was Isaiah smiling as he was putting on a tae kwon do uniform—they call it a tobok, I think—and being shown how to wear his white belt. Then he joined the group on the floor."

Isaiah showed up bright and early Saturday morning, eager as always to get right to work. Chip was thinking about the game with Southwestern that afternoon, but he took time to talk to Isaiah about the Y and tae kwon do class. Toward noon, football fever seemed to grip everyone who came into Grayson's. Then the tension even gripped Chip.

Come on, Chip chided himself. *Cut this out! You'll be a wreck before the game even starts!*

Chip wasn't the only one who was tense. Every football fan in the state knew Southwestern was the big test. Not that anyone expected a miracle. One game didn't make a season. Not with Cathedral, Midwestern,

NOW IT'S UP TO THE KIDS

Grantland, Wesleyan, and A & M yet to come. But Southwestern had won the Sugar Bowl game, and nearly every starter was back. If the kids from State could make a good showing, it would sure help.

Yes, football was in the air and on the tip of every tongue in University. And, naturally, it was all Southwestern.

"They outweigh us by twenty pounds a man on the line!"

"Same thing in the backfield!"

"Beat Brandon thirty to nothing!"

"They'll run Ralston's sophomores right out of the stadium! Remember last year? Remember the trouncing they gave us? It'll be worse this afternoon!"

"I just don't follow Ralston's reasoning of trying to play big-time football with a bunch of kids!"

It was impossible for the players to escape all the adulation for Southwestern. They heard "Sugar Bowl Heroes" at every turn; they heard Southwestern on the streets and in the restaurants and in the stores and on the radio and TV and read about the team's great prowess in every newspaper.

Curly Ralston, Henry Rockwell, Jim Sullivan, and the rest of the coaches caught it too. They heard all the tributes and read all the raves; but it was old stuff to them, and they shrugged it off. It meant nothing to them personally, but that didn't mean they didn't worry about the effect on the players. Ralston paced restlessly back and forth in the coaches' room while the team was dressing. Suddenly, he turned to Sullivan. "Take a turn through the locker room, Jim," he suggested. "See if you can gauge how they feel."

Ralston and Rockwell sat in silence after Sullivan left, each going over in his own mind all the little things a coach reviews before an important game. A strong friendship had developed between these two men who were so different and yet so strongly devoted to the same principles. Ralston broke the silence, his worried frown relaxing slightly as he eyed his first assistant. "Think they'll crack, Rock?"

Rockwell shook his head, his thin lips curling slightly upward as he answered. "No," he grunted, "I don't!"

"How about a little talk before the game? Think they need it?"

Again Rockwell shook his head. "No, Curly," he said quietly, "I think we should treat this game just like any other." He paused briefly and then continued. "They're up. Way up. We've done all we can. Now it's up to the kids!"

Sullivan came tramping up the steps from the locker room, and the two older men eyed the door expectantly. There was a smile on Jim's face when he opened the door and entered the office. "Somebody is in for a rude awakening," he said, "and it isn't going to be us." He dropped lightly into a chair beside the desk. "This is the first time in the memory of man that a State team was all suited up and ready to go twenty minutes ahead of time."

"That means they're ready," Ralston said crisply. "And it means you're right, Rock. They're up! Come on. Let's get 'em out on the field before they explode!"

Chip had dressed quickly. Then, aware of the tension gripping his teammates, he leaned back against the wall and tried to relax, but he couldn't get his thoughts off the game. He nearly jumped out of his uniform when Curly Ralston opened the door and shouted, "Let's go!"

Sixty thousand spectators were in the stadium when nearly one hundred State players ran down the runway and out on the freshly mowed green football field.

NOW IT'S UP TO THE KIDS

Dressed in their home uniforms of spotless white pants with red and blue stripes down the sides, red jerseys with white numerals outlined in blue, and red helmets with a blue "STATE" embossed on each side and a blue stripe outlined in white running down the center from front to back, they looked sharp, ready.

As the players spread across one-half of the field for their stretching and warm-up drills, it seemed to Chip that every person in the place must be cheering for State. Then Southwestern ran out on the field, and the roar sounded even more deafening.

Chip was loosening up his kicking leg, and as he warmed up, he studied the Southwestern players. Their white jerseys with brilliant orange numerals, white pants, and glossy white helmets with a large orange "SW" on each side and an orange stripe running front to back made them seem bigger than their reported weights. But big as they were, Chip noted their speed more. "Big and fast," he muttered. "This is going to be tough."

Chip was right. The visitors were big, fast, and tough—and overconfident. Chip knocked the ball into the end zone on the opening kickoff, and the ball was brought out to the twenty-yard line. Then the visitors clicked off eighty yards in nine plays to score a touchdown and kick the extra point before the game was five minutes old.

State received and advanced to midfield; but the Southwestern defense tightened, and Chip was forced to punt on fourth down. He angled the ball out of bounds on the Southwestern five-yard stripe, but the visitors swung right into high again and marched to the State thirty before giving up the ball on downs.

Throughout the first half, Southwestern was cocky and careless but could do nothing wrong. State was determined and full of fight but could do nothing right. At the half Southwestern led, 13-0.

The tide turned in the second half. State received, and Speed Morris caught the ball on his own five-yard line. He saw a glimpse of daylight straight up the middle and was through the hole and on his way before Chip could say "touchdown." He might have gone all the way, too, except for a weak block by Bebop Leopoulos. Bebop left his feet a split second too soon, and that allowed his man to get a hand on Speed, slowing his momentum. The Southwestern tacklers caught up and spilled Speed on the Southwestern forty.

Chip passed on the first play, faking to Finley on a draw play and firing a hard pass to Higgins on the visitors' fifteen. Larry made it to the ten, and it was first and goal for State in the first minute of the second half. Chip carried the ball himself for three fast strides and then pitched out to Finley. Fireball was forced to the sideline but pegged a hard pass to Whittemore crossing behind the Southwestern safety. Whitty held the ball for the touchdown! Chip looked at the officials to be sure there weren't any flags. Fireball had managed to stay behind the line of scrimmage on his touchdown toss. Chip kicked the extra point. The score: Southwestern 13, State 7.

Southwestern received, and Chip again kicked the ball into the end zone. Then the visitors got careless and tried to get the seven points back in a hurry. Held for no gain on two running plays, the quarterback tried a pass out into the flat, but Speed Morris came from nowhere to snare the ball and dart across the goal line untouched for another State touchdown. Chip again kicked the extra point, and the big scoreboard showed State ahead, 14-13, with only three minutes gone in the second half.

NOW IT'S UP TO THE KIDS

The game turned into a real battle. Southwestern was scared and turned up the pressure all over the field, but State fought right back. Then the visitors got a big break. After an exchange of punts, the Southwestern quarterback lofted a high, fifty-yard pass that Wynn Burnett deflected, but the ball landed smack into the hands of the visitors' surprised right end in the end zone. The try for the extra point was good, and Southwestern led, 20-14.

Lightning did strike twice in the same place, and football breaks cared nothing about personalities. Captain Mike Brennan elected to receive, and Ralston alternated Speed Morris and Fireball Finley with Wynn Burnett as return men. The visitors' kicker booted the ball high and long and straight to Wynn Burnett. Southwestern was succeeding in keeping the ball away from the ever-dangerous Speed Morris and Fireball Finley. Wynn dropped back a few steps, concentrated on the ball until it stuck in his hands, and then started upfield at full speed. He got off to a fast start and sped across the twenty, the thirty, and up to the forty-yard line before he was hit. Then he fumbled!

Southwestern recovered, faked a draw play, and scored on a rifle pass to the same right end. The tall receiver fought with Wynn Burnett for the ball and won the tussle for another touchdown. Burnett was so angry because of the play that he took himself out of the game. Ralston substituted Junior Roberts and met Wynn at the sideline. He tried to console Burnett, who was in a frenzy. The home fans were stunned by the suddenness of the break, but they gave Wynn an understanding cheer.

Biggie Cohen broke through the line like a mad bull to make the placekicker hurry the try for the extra point, and the ball flew wide of the goal. But McCarthy was offsides, and the second try was good. That made the score 27-14, and State's hopes dimmed.

When the referee gave Captain Mike Brennan his choice, Mike surprised everyone by electing to have State kick off after the Southwestern score. "Gotta get the ball down in their end of the field somehow!" he growled.

Before State could line up for the kick, the quarter ended and the teams changed goals. Chip's kick was high and down to the Southwestern five-yard line, where Finley dropped the receiver before he had taken three steps. The State fans liked the bone-crushing tackle and began to chant "Fight, team, fight! Fight, team, fight!"

It may have been the "fight" cheer or the sight of the game clock ticking away State's championship hopes. Whatever it was, it brought results. Tiny Tim McCarthy and Mike Brennan and Soapy Smith and Biggie Cohen and Joe Maxim tore through the Southwestern line and chased the ballcarrier across the goal line for a safety. But it was small consolation. The clock showed twelve minutes to play with the score Southwestern 27, State 16.

Southwestern had to put the ball in play from its twenty-yard line by a free kick, which could be a punt, a placekick, or a drop kick. The visitors elected to place-kick, and Finley snared the ball at the State's thirty and carried it back to the visitors' forty-five.

Chip hit Whittemore with a buttonhook pass that was good for ten and a first down, and then Southwestern held three straight times. It was fourth and eight with the ball on the visitors' thirty-three-yard line. In the huddle, Chip called for a pass, but Brennan interrupted him. "Kick it, Chip!" Mike urged. "Kick the field goal! I've got a hunch!"

Chip hesitated and Brennan continued. "They're tired, Chip. If you kick it, they'll receive, and we'll take it away from them again. I've got the feeling. I know we'll do it! Right, guys?"

"I'm not sure, Mike. If I miss the field goal, they'll get the ball in good field position," Chip warned.

"I know we can do it," Mike affirmed.

Chip didn't like it, but he changed the call, and State came out of the huddle in field-goal formation. That brought a groan from the State fans and some derisive remarks from the opponents.

"What goes? You guys afraid of a little contact football?"

"Now I've seen everything! Eleven points behind and they try for a field goal from fifty yards! Yeah, right! Good-bye game!"

"Who's callin' the plays for you guys—the student managers?"

As fast as the same grouchy fan could say "snap, spot, kick," State had three more points on the board! With Speed holding, Chip booted a perfect placement, and that made the score Southwestern 27, State 19. The visitors received, and veteran Mike Brennan dropped the receiver in his tracks on the Southwestern eight-yard line. His vicious tackle seemed to set the pattern. Three straight times Cohen, McCarthy, and Maxim fought through the visitors' offensive line as if it were made of paper, forcing the ball back to the four-yard line. That made it fourth and fourteen.

Fireball beckoned to Speed and backed up to mid-field, hoping Speed or he would have a chance to make a good run back. But he got a better break. Biggie crashed through the line and knocked the backfield blocker, the ball, and the punter in three different directions, giving Silent Joe Maxim the chance to fall on the ball in the end zone for a touchdown.

The State fans nearly tore down the stadium when the referee threw his arms overhead to designate the score. And they were still in a frenzy when Chip booted another extra point. That made the score Southwestern 27, State 26, with five minutes left to play.

Chip turned after the kick and moved over beside Biggie Cohen. "We've got to have the ball, Biggie," he said. "Remember our old Valley Falls onside kick? I'm going to try it! Tell Whittemore to block their tackle out, and you block the guard in. I'll tell Speed. He'll get the ball. OK?"

Cohen nodded grimly. "We'll take care of the blocking," he muttered. "You tell Speed he better get that ball!" He turned away but hesitated long enough to say, "Now you're doin' some *real* quarterbacking!"

Mike Brennan was jubilant, clapping his teammates on the back and challenging them to make the kickoff tackle. "We've got 'em back on their heels *now*," he exulted. "Let's go get 'em! Let's get that ball! What d'ya say, guys? Give us a high, long kick, Chip!"

Chip was tempted to tell Mike about the onside kick, but he didn't want to tip off the Southwestern players lining up outside their restraining line. The execution of an onside kick required perfect deception; everything, but everything, had to point to an anticipated downfield boot. So Chip remained silent, praying he could execute his part accurately and that Speed, Biggie, and Whitty would do the rest.

Brennan had his teammates steamed up, all right. If it was deception Chip was worried about, they eliminated that item pronto. On Chip's kick, they charged down the field and through the visitors as if they were sprinting a hundred-yard dash—that is, all but Cohen, Whittemore, and Morris.

NOW IT'S UP TO THE KIDS

The dashing wave of players fooled Southwestern, the fans, and the officials as well. Suddenly, they saw the slithering ball bouncing along the ground past the Southwestern restraining line, right between Cohen and Whittemore. Then they saw two of the best blocks ever thrown in any football game, and the way was clear for Speed Morris to dive on the ball and enfold it under his curled-up body.

It took a second for the fans to understand what they had witnessed, but then they were on their feet, their programs, empty Coke cups, and red-and-blue confetti flying. The referee was standing over Speed and pointing toward the Southwestern goal. It was State's ball first and ten, on its forty-five yard line with four minutes and fifty seconds to play.

Chip's teammates were completely mystified. "What happened?" Brennan demanded. "Bad kick?" He was panting heavily after his mad dash down the field and looked from Chip to Speed to Cohen to Whittemore and back to Chip for the explanation.

"We'll tell you later," Chip said. "Come on now. This is our big chance!"

The Southwestern captain was a veteran of many close and tough games and immediately took a time-out. That gave Chip a chance to work up a sequence of plays, and when time was in, his teammates knew exactly what was coming. And they clicked! An over-the-line toss to Higgins was good for five, Fireball hit through the middle for three, and Speed darted over tackle on a quick-opener for three more and the first down. Now it was first and ten on the Southwestern forty-four-yard line, and the cheer "We want a touchdown" came booming in toward the two teams from every direction.

Chip darted straight back from the center, faked a

handoff to Fireball driving through the middle, faked another to Speed on the way, and raised the ball as if for a long pass. Just when it seemed the charging visitors would throw him for a loss, he flipped an underhand pass to Whittemore cutting around behind his own line. Whitty broke through a hole inside the Southwestern end and carried to the twenty for another first down. Southwestern called another time-out.

In the huddle, Chip ran through his plans, thankful for the extra time. "We can't risk an interception now, guys," he said. "We'll stick with running plays and try to keep in the center of the field."

Brennan patted Chip on the back. "That's the ticket, Chipper." He looked around the circle of faces. "This is our big break, guys. Chip is figuring on a field goal if we can't gain. Right, Chip? That means we've got to hold that line if he has to try for the three-pointer." He thrust out his hand. "This is our chance, guys. Let's do it!"

Southwestern stiffened, and after three plays, the ball rested on the fifteen-yard line, practically in the center of the field. The bedlam was deafening now, but it didn't bother the State players. It wasn't necessary for Chip to call the signals in the huddle. He simply extended his hand and every player joined in the team clasp, each determined to do his job.

While his teammates were in the huddle, Speed moved up to a position six and a half yards behind the ball and carefully knelt down and scanned the path he expected Chip's toe to travel. When the team broke out of the huddle and moved up to the ball, Southwestern was already dug in, prepared to charge. There wasn't any question in the opponents' minds about the possibility of a kick.

Chip concentrated on the spot and called the signals.

NOW IT'S UP TO THE KIDS

On the count of three, the ball came spinning back, and Speed plopped it down as if it were merely a practice kick instead of one that meant another long step toward the conference championship.

Chip's job was routine. He booted the ball quickly and surely. It whirled end over end and over the goal, splitting the posts for a perfect three-pointer. State led, 29-27, with a minute left to play, and the stands erupted like a volcano, spilling fans and spectators down to the all-weather track and out near the sidelines circling the field.

Southwestern received, and Chip booted the ball clear over the end zone and into the crowd of fans. That left fifty seconds to play and time for Southwestern to try three passes from their own twenty. All of them sputtered, incomplete. State fans were counting down the seconds.

Before the quarterback could get the ball in play for a last desperate pass, the game clock hit 00:00, the whistle shrilled, and State had won its big game!

CHAPTER 11

The Powerful and Positive Force

MAIN STREET had been the scene of many victory parades during the years State had been located in University. But none could equal the spontaneous celebration after the Southwestern victory. Crowds had formed on the field right after the game and eventually made their way downtown. By the time Chip and his teammates reached the business section of the city, Main Street was a boiling mass of frenzied football faithfuls.

"You'd think we'd won the national championship," Soapy quipped.

Grayson's had lines coming out the door, but the guys managed to get through the mob and slip through the side entrance on Tenth Street. Few of the celebrants recognized their football heroes. Soapy lowered a shoulder and did his best blocking of the day as he plowed a path back to the employee lounge. Slipping quickly into the standard-issue Grayson's "uniform"—red-and-blue polo shirt and white slacks—Soapy fought his way to the fountain, loudly proclaiming, "Business must continue as usual, ladies and gentlemen, regardless of the limited staff on hand to meet this unusual demand."

The crowd promptly recognized the football heroes when they appeared in their working attire. Then the commotion reached such proportions that James "Pop" King, a member of the special-event security group for the day's game, ambled in and jokingly threatened to "have everyone hauled downtown." The wise old policeman worked the day shift as a twenty-five-year veteran of the University police force and had been through all this many times through the years. When he saw no one was interested in his joking, he made his way to the back of Grayson's where he could get a better view.

Fireball spotted Pop in the back of the noisy room and ushered his policeman friend into the stockroom where Chip was talking to Isaiah and Mark.

"Chip," Fireball interrupted, "this is Pop King." He paused and then continued pointedly, "Pop knows Tenth Street inside and out. Well, gotta run. See you later, Pop."

Chip shook his hand and started to introduce Isaiah and Mark, but King stopped him. "I already know these two," King said, ruffling Mark's hair. "They live in my district. I'm off duty and just helping out over here as game security today because of the crowd." He gestured toward Isaiah. "How's this young fellow making out on the job?"

"He's doing all right," Chip said warmly. "He's a good worker."

King studied Chip appreciatively. "You guys are showing up those so-called experts, aren't you?"

Chip smiled. "I guess we're pretty fortunate."

"Not from what I hear," King said.

"Chip won the game!" Mark bragged. "I watched it on TV."

"Want to do me a favor, Isaiah, and Mark?" Chip interrupted. "See if you can get me a paper."

When the brothers set out on their mission, Chip turned to Pop. "Mr. King, do you have a couple of minutes?"

King laughed. "With that mob out there? I sure do! I'm sitting right here until they run out of energy or until George Grayson runs out of food for them. Now you go ahead, young man. What's up?"

"I wanted to talk to you about that crowd of kids that hangs out on Tenth Street outside the pizza place. The ones Isaiah and Mark sometimes hang around with."

King shook his head. "Oh, them! That isn't a crowd; that's a gang of young hoods. Not the little ones now. Not the little guys like Mark. And not the naive followers like Isaiah. But the rest of them, well, they're headed in the wrong direction. What's on your mind?"

"Well, Isaiah has been having trouble with one or two of the bigger ones, and I'd like to help him. The trouble is, I don't know how to go about it."

King nodded understandingly. "I know," he said, "I know. Isaiah Redding is a nice kid, but he's been hanging around that corner crowd for the last few months and now he's nearly like one of them, like the other kids in that neighborhood."

"But don't their parents try to keep them at home?"

"Son," King said kindly, "the people who live in that area are pretty discouraged. When they reach the stage that they have to live in that section, they've just about hit bottom. I've chased off that core bunch of kids a hundred times. But soon as I turn *my* back, *they're* back! If the parents would cooperate, I might be able to do something. But they won't, or can't, or else they haven't got time, and the kids are just about out of hand."

"I guess you know Tony Carlara and Bucky Husta."

King nodded grimly. "I know them well enough. Too well! Not bad kids at heart, at least Tony isn't, but the way they're going, there is only one destination—trouble!"

"They seem to have Isaiah scared to death. At least that's the impression I get, and I don't like it. Do you think I can help him in any way? I'd like to help the whole bunch if I could. How about the Police Athletic League? Can they do anything?" Chip asked.

"Well," King drawled, "yes and no. If we could get a little cooperation from the parents and the kids themselves, we could do a lot. So far, we haven't had a bit of luck in that neighborhood.

"Tell you what, Chip. Why don't you go see Lieutenant Byrnes of the Juvenile Delinquent Division? He's down at 1967 Main Street. He's the recreational director of the P. A. L. Youth Center and knows most of the answers. Does a fine job. He's a great sports fan, and I know he'd be happy to meet you. I'll tell him you're coming down. Well, guess I'd better get back on the job. Let me know how you make out. So long."

Isaiah came in with the paper right after Pop King left, and for the first time, Chip noticed how down he seemed. But he was wise enough not to comment until he could get a chance to talk to Mark. His opportunity came when Soapy sent for more syrups and other fountain supplies and Isaiah left to fill the order. Then he turned to Mark. "What's wrong with Isaiah now?"

"Bucky jumped him again this morning."

"Why?"

"Because he joined the Y."

"What's wrong with joining the Y?"

"Nothing, I guess, except none of the guys from our neighborhood go there."

"What happened?"

"Well, Bucky caught Isaiah going home and told him to stay away from the Y. Isaiah said he wouldn't do it, and they got into another fight. Then Tony came along and broke it up. Then Bucky and Tony had an argument, and Tony asked Bucky if he wanted to make something of it, and Bucky backed down."

"*That's* different," Chip observed dryly.

"Lots of things are gonna be different," Mark boasted. "Feel my muscle. I'm gonna train at the Y too! I'll take care of that Bucky! Just you wait! I'm gonna get good at that condo stuff—"

"It's tae kwon do, Mark."

"Well, whatever it is."

"How did Bucky find out about Isaiah joining the Y?"

Mark shrugged. "Tony and Bucky find out about everything."

Isaiah came back then, and Chip dropped the subject. Later, after the rush outside quieted down, Soapy came back with extra thick shakes for Isaiah and Mark. When they'd polished them off, Chip sent the two boys home.

After work that night, Chip, Soapy, Fireball, and Whitty walked down Tenth Street to Pete's Restaurant for a midnight snack. Chip was enjoying the privilege of being able to relax and take his time, secure in the knowledge that there was no eleven o'clock football curfew to worry about that night.

Pete was thrilled to have the State football stars in his restaurant and introduced Chip and his teammates to every customer in the place. Everyone joined in the football conversation, and when Pop King came in at midnight, the customers were still at it.

THE POWERFUL AND POSITIVE FORCE

Soapy was right on the job Sunday morning, rousing his friends and presenting each with a copy of the *Herald* opened to the sports section. He made a point of drawing the attention of each sleepy friend—and Chip Hilton in particular—to Bill Bell's story about the game.

"Bell says we're the greatest, Chip," Soapy exulted. "He calls you 'Mister Toe'! Says we're gonna win the conference and that we're a cinch for one of the bowl games. Now what do you think about that?

"Oh, yes, it says here that Chip Hilton is gonna make all-conference, and he wouldn't be surprised if Chip was an all-American. Says Chip has his vote right now whether or not we win another game!"

Chip couldn't take it. He dressed quickly and started for church. After the service he took a long walk and had lunch at Pete's, where he read the sports pages of the *Herald* word for word. He saw what Soapy had neglected to mention. He read with a smile the short blurb on the University High School girls' soccer match. Leah Cahill had scored her first goal of the season in a come-from-behind victory over Rocky River. Then Chip went back to Jefferson Hall and took a nap. After dinner he hit the books, caught up on weekend E-mails to friends, called home, and went to bed at ten o'clock.

Monday between classes, Chip decided it would be a good time to visit the Police Athletic League Youth Center. He told the officer at the desk his name was Chip Hilton and that he would like to see Lieutenant Byrnes.

The stern expression on the man's face disappeared as soon as he heard "Hilton." He smiled broadly and extended his hand. "I'm sure glad to know you, Hilton. Thought I recognized you, but I wasn't sure without that number 44 jersey. Come on, the boss will be happy to see you. You get banged up any on Saturday?"

Chip assured the officer he was fine, and then he was in a big office and facing a man built like a fullback who rose to his feet and crushed his fingers in a firm handclasp.

"Sit down, Chip. Pop King said you'd be around to see me. Now, before we get around to anything else, let's talk a little football. Make yourself comfortable there. You sit down, too, Bill.

"Maybe I don't look it, but I played a little football myself. Yes sir, right here at University High School. Played fullback for three years. Was all-state the last year. I should have gone to college. Had a lot of coaches wanting me to come to their schools. Too smart though. You know how it is with kids—think we know it all. I wanted to get a job and get married. Got the job, got married, and I have a couple of fullbacks of my own at home right now! They're going to be better than their old man too!

"Let's see. You've won four in a row now. Hmmm. Guess the only team you've got to worry about now is A & M. They're tough! Won, let's see, thirteen in a row. I'm going to see that game. Going to take my whole family! Already have tickets, which were hard to get!

"Now, let's see. Pop King said you wanted to do something about a corner crowd down on Tenth, off of Main. Right? Now, how can I help?"

Chip told Byrnes about Tony and Bucky and the difficulty Isaiah apparently was having with the corner crowd. "Pop tells me Isaiah is a good kid, Lieutenant, and I'd like to help him. But I don't know how to go about it."

"I'm familiar with the neighborhood. Pop King knows it better than anyone else, of course. Anyway, it's a tough place to grow up and often as tough to escape. Most of the kids are all right, but they're at an impressionable age, easily led, and apt to get into trouble if the leadership is bad."

"I don't believe the leadership is too good."

"It seldom is, Chip. We've been trying to make some progress in that neighborhood for years. Most of our difficulty has been caused by the constant moving in and out of the residents over the years. The people who dig their roots in down there fall into two groups: the old-timers who've been there for years and who are still attached to the neighborhood and those who don't really have any ties there but can't afford to live anywhere else at the moment.

"In most areas of the community, we can find men and women volunteers who are glad to help solve their neighborhood problems and make them a better place to live. But down there, the people are discouraged and often broke and too busy scrambling to make a living to care much about anything else."

"Don't the kids themselves want something better?"

"Sure they do. Kids from that sort of a neighborhood are pretty much like kids anywhere—they have dreams, want friends, and all the rest. But, often, they don't get the direction or discipline or love from parents that structured much of my life and probably yours too. I find that's where some of the biggest problems come in; some of these kids seek other avenues to fill those needs that they are missing. The family is the basic unit of society. When that falls apart, problems emerge, especially with kids."

Chip listened intently as Byrnes continued.

"You know, it's odd. Kids say they want to be independent individuals, but they keep trying to fit in with a group; and if the family isn't the group providing the direction, love, guidance, and faith, then they'll seek somewhere else to belong.

"And that takes us to your corner crowd. The leader is usually a strong, aggressive kid who can beat up anyone else in the bunch, or else he's a little smarter and has more leadership. The whole deal is based on each kid's hope of being a member of a group for personal protection, belonging, and, in the case of the leader, self-esteem. He wants to be feared, envied, and able to have power over others."

That description sure fits Tony and Bucky, Chip thought.

"Now," Byrnes continued, "that sort of thing spreads through the whole bunch and to all the kids in the neighborhood. The individual members of the group feel strong because they're members of a group or a club or some kind of a secret society or whatever you want to call it."

"Don't they like sports?"

"Of course. But the big thing with these corner gangs is personal strength and the ability to fight. The one person they respect and admire most is the rough-and-tough fighter."

Chip was thinking if he could only show them—prove to them—that they didn't have to be a bully or a braggart to be strong as an individual. "Can't the police do something about the kids hanging around the corners all evening?"

"We, and I mean the police, have tried to get a curfew law here for years. But we've never had much success. It will probably surprise you, but most of the opposition comes from the parents themselves. Ultimately, our success will probably come when we're able to reach the parents and can convince them how powerful and positive a force they can be in their children's lives and in their neighborhoods."

CHAPTER 12

Shakes and Shiners

CHIP LEARNED a great deal about the aims and objectives of the Police Athletic League from Lieutenant Byrnes, and he learned a lot about the challenges adults experience in attempting to help impressionable preteens and teenagers with their vital problems. But he hadn't found the answer to Isaiah Redding's situation, and when he reached Grayson's, he ran face first into it again. Isaiah was standing on the scales, his bony shoulders slumped forward and little chin held up by his chest, while Soapy moved the scale weights. Chip paused in the doorway.

"What's going on, big man?" Soapy inquired, slapping Isaiah on the back.

"I haven't been eating too much at home lately," Isaiah said weakly, his voice barely audible.

"No change since the last weigh-in," Soapy said, ruffling Isaiah's hair. "Come on," he urged. "Let's get that chin up and get on the ball. Let's see, it's eight o'clock. We'll have another fruit shake. If we're going to make an athlete out of you, we've all got to work together. You have to do your part. You gotta eat right at home too."

He looked up and saw Chip. "Isaiah's down again, Chip," he said quietly. "Real down."

"He'll snap out of it," Chip said casually. "Don't worry about Isaiah."

Soapy went back to the counter, and Chip and Isaiah worked on the stockroom inventory. While they worked, Chip tried to draw him out. But Isaiah wasn't talking, and Chip gave up and concentrated on the job. But his concentration was interrupted. Soapy opened the door and with his arm draped across Mark's shoulder, guided the little boy into the stockroom.

"Look, Chip, look at this!" Soapy said, pointing to Mark's eye. "Look at Mark's shiner!"

Mark had a beauty. His eye was black above, on the lids, below and halfway down his cheek.

"What happened to you?" Chip gasped.

"Must run in the family," Soapy quipped.

"Don't run in the family," Mark said ominously. "Just wait! Wait until I learn that condo stuff!"

"That's tae kwon do," Chip corrected gently.

Mark measured Chip speculatively. "Tae kwon do," he repeated carefully. "My way was easier. Well," he continued, "we going to talk or work?"

"Isaiah and I are going to work," Chip said decisively. "You're going to do some reading. Right over there at that desk. Here's a book I got you from the library. Now get busy!"

Soapy couldn't understand it. He came back to the stockroom repeatedly, bringing an ice-cream cone for Mark, a fruit shake for Isaiah, and a Coke for Chip. But it didn't work. Chip wasn't talking, and he wouldn't let Isaiah or Mark talk.

SHAKES AND SHINERS

On the way home after work, Soapy couldn't stand it any longer. "How did Mark get that black eye?" he asked.

"I don't know."

"You don't know!" Soapy repeated. *"Didn't you ask?"*

"No, Soapy, I didn't."

Soapy began grumbling about that being no way to help a kid—no, two kids—who needed help and he was surprised by some people's attitude and that it didn't seem possible that a guy's best friend would be so mysterious about something they were both so interested in.

Chip let Soapy continue to rant, but just before they reached Jeff, he explained that he felt the best way to help Isaiah right now was to wait and see if the boy could work his way out of his troubles on his own. "Let's wait and see what happens, Soapy. In the meantime, I've got to come up with some idea, some sort of a plan, so I can win over that corner crowd."

The days passed, and Chip was no closer to a solution. Isaiah was still down, but every night he and Mark went to the Y at seven o'clock for tae kwon do classes. All that week University buzzed with football talk: the conference championship, the Rose Bowl, the Sugar Bowl, the Cotton Bowl, the Orange Bowl, the Peach Bowl, and all the other bowl games.

Friday came, and just before Chip started for University Stadium for the team's departure for the Cathedral game, Soapy weighed Isaiah.

"Chip! A hundred and three pounds! A heavyweight!"

Students, townspeople, professors, fans, and players crowded around the team buses, cheering, yelling, and holding up posters of support. The band members were spread around the area, blasting out the State University fight song. It was a charged scene filled with music, color, and optimism at its greatest intensity. When the buses pulled out, State's varsity was aboard, with all the players thrilled by the send-off and determined to justify the fans' faith the next afternoon against Cathedral. And they did!

State won in the first ten minutes of the game. Cathedral won the toss, received, and fumbled on the second play. It was State's ball on the Cathedral thirty, and the Statesmen scored on the first play, with Chip lofting a high pass to Larry Higgins in the end zone for the tally. He kicked the extra point and State led, 7-0.

Cathedral received again, carried to the twenty-five, couldn't gain, and was forced to punt. Fireball Finley took the kick on the State forty-five and brought it back to the Cathedral forty. Then Chip used his hidden-ball faking ability and sent Morris streaking through left tackle and all the way across the goal line. It was as easy as that, and Ralston began freely substituting. Chip's scoring was limited to four extra points and a twenty-yard field goal. The final score registered State 31, Cathedral 14. It could have been much higher had Coach Ralston not given the second and third strings an opportunity to play the entire second half.

Traveling back to University, the team learned that A & M had won its fourteenth-straight game in a non-conference contest over Riordon, 39-6. But the players forgot that news when the buses rolled into University. It seemed to Chip that the band and the fans must have waited right there all night. This time, however, there was a little more organization.

After the sleepy-eyed athletes tumbled off the buses, Ralston spoke briefly, remarking that a good team never looked over its shoulder and that one victory or five victories didn't make a season. "We are meeting the Dukes next Saturday. They are one of the best teams, if not the best, in the country, and we'll have to work hard. Thanks to everyone for coming out to welcome your team home."

Chip spent that Sunday as he did almost every Sunday, taking a walk to limber up, going to church, E-mailing friends, calling his mom in Valley Falls, and studying.

The next afternoon, he had lunch with Tims Lansing and then spent two hours in the library doing research for an English paper before practice. When he got to work, Lieutenant Byrnes was chatting with the unattainable light of Soapy's life, Mitzi Savrill, Grayson's beautiful cashier.

"Hello, Chip. Nice win! Tough one coming up Saturday?"

"Everyone says they're good, Mr. Byrnes."

"You'll take 'em," Byrnes said confidently. "Is there a place where we can talk? Got time?"

"Sure," Chip said, smiling at Mitzi. "Come on back to the best office in the place, the stockroom."

Byrnes made himself comfortable in the desk chair. "How's your protégé working out?"

"Fine, on the job."

"What kind of a kid is he?"

"Isaiah's a good kid, Mr. Byrnes."

Byrnes nodded. "Yes, they're all good kids until they get mixed up with some wise guy who talks them into a lot of trouble. It's the same old story of the company a kid keeps—the one bad apple in the barrel."

Chip interjected. "Isaiah isn't going to be led into trouble, but he might be bullied into doing something he doesn't want to do. I'd like to get to know the kids on that corner, but—they're not very receptive."

"It's not you. You're no exception," Byrnes said dryly. "This town is like a lot of college towns, Chip. And the kids here in University are like lots of college-town kids. Sometimes there's friction between the local kids—even the adults—and the college students. College students are often stereotyped and perceived as having money, cars, and nice clothes, not to mention opportunities that seem unreachable by some of the local kids."

"You're sure not talking about me," Chip smiled ruefully. "Nor many of the ones I know. A lot of us college kids work at something."

Byrnes nodded. "I know. But the kids I'm talking about don't realize that. Let's not forget, though, some college kids do have all those things and show it.

"Now back to the kids. We've never had any success in organizing a PAL team or group in that neighborhood." He shrugged wryly. "Right where we need it most. Tell you what. Suppose I ask Pop King to come in? I saw him heading down Tenth Street just a few minutes ago and asked him to stick around until I saw you. Got time to talk a little longer?"

"I sure have and I really appreciate your help."

"Kids are my business, Chip, big ones and little ones too. I'll be right back."

A few minutes later, Byrnes returned with King. "Pop, we've been talking about the kids on Tenth. Chip says you know about it."

King nodded. "I know about it, all right. I've hoofed that neighborhood for going on thirty years, and I guess I know every man, woman, and kid down there. And I know those kids you're talking about. They're tough."

King waved a hand. "Now, don't get me wrong. I don't

mean they're bad kids. But they're wide open for bad influences. One thing is sure, Tony and Bucky will be easy prey for the first real tough one who comes along. Right now, they're beginning to show dislike for authority and discipline and anyone or anything that represents it. They've got every kid in the neighborhood buffaloed."

"Do you think they've got some kind of hold on Isaiah?"

King nodded grimly. "They've got a hold on every kid in that neighborhood, Chip. Without knowing it, you probably got Isaiah in trouble with Tony and Bucky just because you went to see him. They've got no use for college boys or outsiders, and they won't put up with a kid from their neighborhood having anything to do with their prejudices."

"But we work together!"

"Means nothing. You're still a college student and an outsider. They probably beat him up Sunday five minutes after you left."

"But why doesn't he tell someone? His father, you, or me, or anyone?"

King grimaced. "Tell someone? You mean snitch or squeal? That would be breaking or going against the unwritten code and being disloyal to their own. You've got as much chance of getting one of those kids to talk as that chair. Forget *that!*"

"What about school? And teams and parties and things like that?"

"For some, school is the place to meet their friends and hang out. For others, school is the foundation for later years, and for still others, it's both. Unfortunately, some of the corner kids are just waiting until they're old enough to quit school, find a job, or maybe hang around, and eventually get into trouble.

"Then, someday, a real tough one, or some older guy who thinks he's cool, comes along, and they fall for his line and he takes over, and then there's real trouble."

"But there must be *some way* to make a difference," Chip protested. "How about sports? Couldn't they get the kids playing baseball and basketball?"

Byrnes answered that question. "We've tried to organize teams down there time and again, but we've never had any luck. If we had a community house or a center of some kind in that neighborhood, it would help."

Lieutenant Byrnes and Pop King left a little later. Chip was frustrated and discouraged. If Byrnes and King didn't know the answer, there wasn't much chance for him to solve Isaiah Redding's problem. Maybe he could, if he could only do something to change Tony Carlara and Bucky Husta.

His thoughts were interrupted by a knock on the door. Mitzi was uncharacteristically embarrassed. "Chip," she said timidly, "will you do me a big favor?" Without waiting for an answer she plunged in, speaking hurriedly. "I guess everyone is asking you to get tickets for them, but honest, Chip, I've tried to get them everywhere."

Chip smiled. "You want tickets? Is that all? You'll get tickets! How many?"

"I . . . I want an awful lot—"

"How many?" Chip interrupted.

"Well, I have my own, of course, but if I could get three more—"

"You'll have them. That's one advantage of making varsity. We get complimentary tickets, and we can reserve more for every game. We have to pay for the regular tickets, of course, with the demand the way it is. I never use mine anyway, except when my mom or a few of the guys from Valley Falls come up for a game."

SHAKES AND SHINERS

"Great! Thanks, Chip, this is a real favor."

Chip made a note to himself about Mitzi's tickets. Right then he had an inspiration! This was it! Now he had the answer. At least a start toward it. He'd try to get Tony and Bucky and some of the others interested in football with tickets to the games!

Soapy, Fireball, Biggie, Red, Speed, and Whitty weren't using all their passes, and they would be glad to let him have them if it would help Isaiah and Mark.

That evening Isaiah was a little brighter. Soapy got him on the scales, and he weighed in at 105 pounds. At the first opportunity, Chip brought up his football ticket idea. "Do you think Tony and Bucky and some of the other guys in your neighborhood would like to see the game with the Dukes on Saturday, Isaiah?"

Isaiah shook his head. "I don't know, Chip. I don't think so."

"You and Mark are going, aren't you?" Chip asked.

"Yes," Isaiah said reluctantly. "Mark wants to go awful bad."

"How about Tony and Bucky? Do you want to ask them to go?"

Isaiah's indecisive attitude was enough for Chip. "Never mind," he said understandingly. "I'll ask them myself."

CHAPTER 13

Big-Time Football

CHIP WAS really in good spirits and eager when he reported for practice Tuesday afternoon. Everything seemed to be working out the way he wanted. He had gotten the tickets for Mitzi, and he had accumulated enough complimentary player tickets from his teammates for Tony and Bucky and the corner crowd. Chip's teammates were up too. Every player on the squad seemed anxious to get going. It was a practice session that brought out the coaches' smiles.

It was a fast-paced workout, and Ralston was pleased. He sent the players to the showers and was waiting when they assembled in the meeting room. "Nice going, men," he said, nodding his head. "That kind of a workout warms a coach's heart. Now, I want to turn this meeting over to Coach Sullivan. He knows more about the Grantland Dukes than their whole coaching staff does. Jim, it's all yours."

Jim Sullivan spoke with authority. He knew exactly

what he was talking about. He diagrammed the Dukes' formation and the spacing of their line and the backs and discussed their plays, the outstanding runners, passers, and receivers. Then he shifted to the defense.

"Their line is terrific," Sullivan emphasized. "If you guys thought Southwestern had a tough line, wait until you see the Dukes. It's the hardest-charging offensive or defensive line I've ever seen. They're bigger, tougher, and smarter than Southwestern.

"Defensively, however, they're built to order for trap plays. Their constant charging should set them up perfectly for our trap series. Coach Ralston and Coach Rockwell will talk over the plays they've worked up, so I won't spend anymore time on that phase of it. I might add right here that they give the passer a tough time. They bust through the line and swarm all over him to get him to rush his passes.

"The Dukes' secondary uses a combination man-to-man and zone defense against passes. Their defensive linebacker calls their signals and tries to mix you up on your blocking assignments by shifting their defensive alignment at the last possible second. Actually, the defense is a 6-2-2-1, shifting into a 5-3-3 when a pass seems imminent.

"My scouting charts show the outside linebackers taking the flat and picking up the ends if they move laterally. Otherwise, these outside linebackers play zone and help out against the short passes. The cornerbacks take the ends every time they cut downfield and stay with them until the ball is in the air. The middle linebacker drops back into the slot and plays zone until a receiver enters the area. Then he plays him man-to-man. If any particular zone is flooded with receivers, the safety man backs it up. He doesn't commit himself until the ball is in the air.

"I noticed that the weak-side end often dropped back and covered his respective flat zone when the passer ran toward the opposite side. If there was no receiver in the flat, he usually dropped straight back into the secondary. Maybe I can present it a little better on the board. All right, Coach?"

Ralston nodded, and Sullivan drew in the Dukes' defense, setting it up against State's unbalanced T-formation. He outlined the 6-2-2-1 defense first and then described the shift into the 5-3-3 pass defense. Then he again discussed the Dukes' offense.

"On offense, as I said before, the line charges hard and fast, which I guess is the reason their ground game is so strong. But they can and will take to the air as a surprise measure. The fullback, number 45, is their best runner and has beaten teams with a pass. He'll attempt some of the throwing against us. The next best runner is Tex Wheat, number 48. He can pass out of the same play as 45 too. Well, I guess that's it, Coach."

Ralston took charge and outlined some of the plays he thought would work against the hard-charging Dukes. Then he excused them with reminders about class attendance, proper rest, and the curfew.

After work that night, Chip walked as far as Pete's Restaurant with his friends. Then he told them that he would meet them later. "Got a little personal business," he said. "Be back in fifteen minutes."

"You're wasting your time," Finley observed, "but we're with you. Good luck!"

The others went into the restaurant, but Soapy stood by the door and watched Chip all the way down the street. When Chip was nearly out of sight, Soapy crossed over to the other side and followed slowly.

Chip fingered the tickets in his pocket as he walked

along, trying to figure out the best way to approach Tony and Bucky. As he drew near the pizza place, he could see the crowd on the corner. It was easy to spot Tony's square figure and Bucky's lanky outline. The two leaders and a crowd of younger kids were deep in an argument, gesturing and talking loudly in boisterous voices. But Tony's quick eyes caught Chip approaching. He muttered something, and the group quieted.

"Hi, Tony. Hi, guys," Chip said, slowing his pace.

Tony eyed Chip warily and kept an invisible wall between them. He made no effort to acknowledge Chip's opening. The boys with him waited tensely, as if these two were boxers sparring for an opening.

"Long time no see," Chip said, his voice calm and sure. "Thought you might drop into Grayson's."

When Tony remained silent, Chip continued. "Anyway I've got some tickets for the game Saturday, and I thought you might want to take it in."

"Game?" Tony repeated slowly. "What game?"

"This Saturday. The game with the Dukes!"

"Never heard of 'em," Tony said slowly. "What kind of a game they play?"

"Football!" someone behind Chip exploded. "Big-time football!"

Tony swung swiftly around. "Who asked you?" he snarled.

Bucky Husta moved behind Chip and in the direction of the speaker. "Yeah," he echoed, "who asked you?"

There was a sudden, tense stillness, and then Chip heard the muffled sound of a body blow. For one brief second Chip was tempted to turn on Bucky. Bucky was crude, and Chip would have gotten between them if Bucky had punched the silenced speaker again; but nothing happened, and Chip concentrated on Tony.

"That's right," he said, "football! The Dukes have one of the best teams in the country. Tickets are sold out. I'd like you guys to come to the game as my guests. What do you say?"

Tony took his time about answering, and Chip continued quickly. "They're on the forty-yard line, almost on the field, Tony. The best in the stadium!"

For a moment Chip thought Tony was going to accept the offer. But after a brief pause, his lips tightened again, and Tony shook his head. "Nah," he said shortly. "We ain't interested in college football. Right, guys?"

The boys backed him up, as Byrnes and King would have predicted, but their response wasn't too enthusiastic. Chip gave it another try. "Suppose I give the tickets to Isaiah. Then if you change your mind, he'll have them for you. OK?"

Tony shrugged. "Whatever. Suit yourself," he said.

"Well, I hope you come," Chip said, turning away. "I know the seats, and I'll stop by to see you."

"Don't bother," Bucky said nastily. "We won't be there!"

Chip said good night and walked away, completely disgusted because he hadn't been able to connect with Tony and his corner followers. "They're impossible," he told himself.

It was ten minutes to eleven when Chip reached Pete's Restaurant. His friends were waiting impatiently on the sidewalk.

"Come on," Soapy urged, "we're late." Then he noted Chip's face. "No luck? I knew it. You're wasting your time."

"I'll say you are," Whittemore added. "Forget about it!"

"I can't forget Isaiah," Chip declared. "Or Mark."

"But you've done everything you could," Fireball argued. "If the PAL can't handle that bunch, I don't see how you figure you're going to do it."

"Look, Chip," Soapy pleaded, "let Isaiah take care of his own trouble. He's lived there two or three years, and nothing serious ever happened to him."

"That's just it," Chip agreed. "He never had any trouble until I gave him the job."

"But that was doing him a favor," Fireball said.

"Oh, sure," Chip said. "It was a favor, all right." He considered a bit and then continued. "One thing is sure! I'm not going to give up and walk away. And, I'm going to find out what makes Tony Carlara and Bucky Husta tick!"

"You'd better forget about the Reddings and start worrying about the Dukes," Finley said pointedly. "Better figure out before Saturday just what makes *them* tick!"

Chip had a lot more help determining what made the Dukes tick than he had in deciding what drove Tony Carlara and Bucky Husta. Curly Ralston, Henry Rockwell, and Jim Sullivan talked about nothing but the Dukes; the three repeated again and again the little scouting tips dealing with false moves, individual player weaknesses and strengths, and the special attacks and defenses the coaches had planned. The earlier raving about Southwestern was nothing compared to their reaction to the mighty Dukes.

That night at work, Chip succeeded in getting Isaiah to take the football tickets—after explaining that he had talked with Tony. "If you can get him to take the tickets, Isaiah, it's all right. And if you can't, it's all right. OK? At any rate, there's two for you and Mark and enough for any of your other friends."

Right afterward, Soapy came rushing in, all excited. Chip waited patiently for him to spring the news. It came when Soapy got Isaiah on the scales.

"Look, Chip, 112 pounds! Another thing! Saturday morning at eleven o'clock Isaiah's going to be in a tae kwon do competition at the Y!"

"Great!" Chip said. "That means he's got to have plenty of sleep. Give him a couple of your shakes and send him home. We'll do the same tomorrow night."

Isaiah hung around a moment. "Er . . . Chip, would you go with me Saturday?"

"We'll all go!" Soapy said gleefully. "We'll be your seconds! Right, Chip? Do they have seconds in tae kwon do, or was I thinking about food again?"

"We've got to back up the champion. Sure we'll go. Now you get out of here and get to bed. All your school work done? How about Mark?"

Coach Ralston ran an efficient and low-key practice on Friday, and everything was set for the mighty Dukes. Chip sent Isaiah home full of shakes and sat down at his desk to review his quarterback instructions. He was completely engrossed in the notes when he heard the sound of running footsteps, and Mark came rushing through the door, panting heavily. A sigh of relief escaped his lips when he saw Chip. "Trouble!" he gasped. "Isaiah's in trouble! You gotta help!"

Soapy was on Mark's heels, his red hair tousled and his voice angry. "What are you doing out this time of night? It's 10:30!"

Mark ignored Soapy and pulled at Chip's arm. "C'mon," he urged. "I'll tell you on the way."

"All right, I'm coming," Chip said uncertainly, glancing at the clock. "But we'll have to hurry. I've got an eleven o'clock curfew." He turned to Soapy. "I'll have to run. See you at the dorm."

Chip and Mark raced out the Tenth Street door, leaving Soapy bewildered by their hurried departure. But only for a second. "Oh, sure!" he muttered, charging toward the fountain.

Mark trotted along at Chip's side, his breath coming in heavy gasps, more from excitement than from the pace.

"Isaiah's taking a truck!" Mark blurted. "Mr. Caruso's truck! Isaiah and Tony and Bucky!"

"What for? Who's Mr. Caruso? Where are they taking the truck?"

"Mr. Caruso owns the pizza place," Mark explained impatiently. "He hauls the store stuff in it. They're gonna take the truck as soon as he closes."

"Where? What for?"

"All I know is Rip and Skids told 'em—" Mark suddenly clapped his hand over his mouth and dropped his head.

"Rip and Skids?" Chip asked gently. "Who are they, Mark?"

But Mark was through talking. At least about Rip and Skids. He ignored the question and pulled Chip into the dark entrance of a building. "We'd better wait here," he whispered. Then he pointed to a dark alley next to the pizza shop. "Down there," he whispered excitedly. "That's where Mr. Caruso keeps the truck. Right beside the basement door. See, he's turning the lights out right now!" He stopped abruptly. "I guess I'd better go home," he said, his voice barely audible. He grasped Chip's arm. "Try to help Isaiah, Chip, please." Then he turned and fled.

CHAPTER 14

Chicken and Curfew

CHIP WAITED uncertainly in the dark, watching Mr. Caruso turn out the lights. Then the little man banged the front door closed, tried the knob, and walked swiftly away in the opposite direction. One light remained on inside the store. In the distance, Chip heard the muffled tones of the student union bell tolling eleven o'clock. "Oh no, now I've done it!" he muttered.

A slight sound drew his attention. A small figure appeared beside the corner of the store and peered up and down the street. Chip recognized Isaiah even in the shadowy darkness. Then a sudden thought struck home. Why wasn't Isaiah home, and where were all the other kids who were usually around the corner? Pop King had said that even when he chased them, they came back and seldom broke up until midnight. And where was Pop King?

Then he heard the starting of an engine. BOOM! A backfire! In the dark stillness, Chip jumped. The engine sputtered and died. Then he heard the engine start again. Chip went into action. He was committed now, whether it was a trap or the real thing. He rushed down the alley just as the engine roared to life. As he ran in front of the truck, the twin headlights pierced the darkness and, for a brief second, caught him in the blinding glare.

Before the driver could push in the clutch and grind the truck into gear, Chip was along the side. He tore open the door and snatched the key out of the ignition, pressing the weight of his right shoulder hard against the boy behind the wheel. Then he turned off the lights and pulled Tony Carlara out on the ground and around in front of the truck.

There was a sudden scurrying on the other side of the seat, and two figures jumped out. But they didn't get far. Someone darted out of the alley at that instant and collared Isaiah and Bucky Husta and pulled them forward, stating fiercely, "Oh, no, you don't!" It was Soapy.

"Where did you come from?" Chip demanded, holding Tony firmly by the shirt. "I thought you went home."

"Without you?" Soapy grunted. "No way! Would Robin leave Batman?" Then he yanked his two prisoners forward. "Now what do we do with them?" he asked.

"We send Isaiah home," Chip said grimly. "And then we walk Tony and Bucky up to the corner for a little talk. Beat it, Isaiah. I'll see you at work in the morning."

"Real nice, Isaiah! Good move!" Soapy said with disgust, shaking Isaiah roughly. "We let you off work so you can get some rest, and this is the thanks—" He shoved Isaiah, and the little guy took off like Fireball Finley returning a kickoff.

Chip grasped Tony by the arm and started up the alley toward Tenth Street. Soapy followed with Bucky.

Suddenly, Bucky tore loose from Soapy's grasp and dashed back down the alley. "You're not takin' me anywhere," he snarled.

"Let him go, Soapy," Chip called, tightening his grasp on Tony. "Tony was driving the truck."

Chip stopped on the corner and backed Tony up against the wall of the pizza place. "Now," he said, holding the truck key in front of Tony's nose, "where did you get this?"

Tony wasn't talking. He pressed his lips together and glared sullenly at the ground. Chip replaced the key in his pocket and grasped Tony by the arm again. "All right," he said firmly, "we'll just take you home and call Pop King and let you explain to him."

That did it. The words spilled out, tumbling one over the other. "You can't do that!" Tony cried. "I wouldn't even get in the door! My dad would go crazy!"

"Then talk! Tell me where you got the key and what you were doing in that truck."

"Caruso hides it—"

"*Mr.* Caruso!"

"Mr. Caruso hides it under the seat. All the guys know that!"

"Is this the first time you tried to take it?"

Tony nodded, his eyes downcast. "Yes," he said, "it's the first time."

"Where were you going with the truck?"

Tony shrugged. "Nowhere. For a ride."

"Do you realize that you were *stealing* the truck?"

Tony shook his head. "He was going to get it back," he said lamely.

"It's still stealing, isn't it? Suppose you ran into a car or hit someone?"

"Yeah," Soapy added fiercely. "Suppose you killed

someone? Think what would happen to you and Isaiah and Bucky. And how about your family!"

"I guess I wasn't thinkin' much," Tony said in a low voice, clearing his throat.

"Where does Mr. Caruso live?" Chip asked.

"Just down the block," Tony said hoarsely. "What are you gonna do?"

"We're going to take the key down to his house and tell him what happened," Chip said. Then he added, "And you're going with us!"

"But—"

"No buts! It's that or else!"

"But he don't like me! He'll call the cops!"

"That's a chance we'll have to take. Come on," Chip said gently. "I don't think he'll be unreasonable. After all, the truck wasn't moved. Don't worry. I'll do the talking."

The Caruso family lived on the first floor of an old brick house. When Chip knocked, the store owner himself cautiously opened the door. "Yes," he said warily, "what is it?"

"Mr. Caruso?" Chip queried.

The little man nodded. "That's me, Frank Caruso." Then he recognized Carlara. "Tony! What's the matter?"

Chip answered the question, handing him the truck key and explaining that Tony had shown them where he lived and that the reason they were on his doorstep was to return the key to his truck.

Frank Caruso didn't understand. "This my key?" he demanded. "What's the matter with my truck?"

Chip told him as clearly as he could that he had surprised some boys in the truck and had chased them away and thought it best to bring the key to the house. "They evidently knew where you kept the key and might have gotten into trouble. Maybe you ought to carry it with you."

Caruso nodded. "Oh, those boys on the corner. They always make trouble!" He nodded grimly toward Tony. "Him too! Thanks, mister. You want to come in? You like some wine?"

Chip declined the friendly invitation and said good night, and the three boys, Tony in the middle, walked back up the street. Chip half expected Tony to break away, but the square-shouldered young leader walked passively along, deep in thought.

Stopping on the corner, Chip gently shook Tony's shoulder. "That wasn't so bad, was it?"

Tony shook his head. "No. Why didn't you tell him about me? Why didn't you tell him I had the key?"

"Because I think you're smart enough to realize that this sort of thing is going to end up only one way: with you in serious trouble, in court, a detention home, out of school, and maybe even in jail."

After a short pause, Chip continued. "And, Tony, because I have confidence in your strength—your strength as an individual. I know you're strong enough to do your own thinking and stand on your own feet. Strong enough to resist the phony leadership of others who want to use you for their dirty work. People like—" Chip paused a long second and then continued. "People like Rip and Skids, for instance. Good night, Tony."

Tony's mouth slacked open in surprise. Long after Chip and Soapy had disappeared up Tenth Street, he stood on the corner by the pizza shop, his hands balled into two hard fists. Then he slowly crossed the street and made his way up the steps of the little house on the corner, slipping softly through the front door.

As soon as they were out of Tony's sight, and almost as if by a signal, Chip and Soapy broke into a run. "Man,

I hope Ralston doesn't hear about this," Soapy said. "Must be 11:30."

"I'm not worrying about him hearing about it," Chip said. "I'm going to tell him."

"Tell him? Are you crazy? He'll throw us off the squad!" When Chip made no reply, Soapy continued. "But Chip, we haven't done anything wrong. It was just the opposite—you were doing something good!"

"Just the same, we broke the rules."

Soapy knew that tone of voice and dropped the subject. They continued in silence, matching strides, and made it to Jeff without incident. But as they started up the steps to the second floor, they met Pete Randolph coming down. Soapy grinned, gave the resident assistant his best smile, and said good night, but Randolph merely grunted.

"He's mad," Soapy muttered. "Everybody in this town is so football crazy they think there's something wrong with you if you don't walk around with a football in your hand."

"All the more reason to tell Coach," Chip said quietly.

Chip wasted no time undressing and getting to sleep, but Soapy kept muttering about the injustice of being an athlete and trying to serve two masters. And why wasn't the curfew twelve o'clock?

Saturdays were big days for the businesses of University. The students were free from classes and descended upon the stores and shops like a tidal wave. But this morning when Chip hurried along Main Street, it wasn't business that occupied the minds of the owners and employees and early customers. It was football! Nothing but football! There were State flags and pennants and painted signs in the windows, along the streets, and adorning the sidewalks. Chip was becoming well known now, and more than one person waved a friendly "hi" to the tall youngster with the blond hair and long strides.

When Chip reached Grayson's, Isaiah was waiting in the stockroom. Isaiah's eyes were downcast, and his whole manner was subdued. Chip said good morning and sat down at the desk, keenly aware that Isaiah was under a terrific strain. Finally, Isaiah broke and walked over to the desk. "I'm sorry, Chip," he said tremulously. "I had to do it."

Isaiah's remorse was obvious, and all of Chip's sympathies were aroused. But he was determined to get to the bottom of the events. "*Why* did you have to do it, Isaiah?" he asked.

"Well, I didn't want to do it. But Tony and Bucky said I was chicken. And, well, no one wants to be chicken."

Chip's blood boiled. "*Chicken!*" he repeated angrily. "What's *chicken* got to do with *stealing* a truck?" He paused and continued contemptuously, "That's a good one! You let someone talk you into stealing a truck to prove you're not chicken! You must have been out of your mind!"

Chip rose from the desk and began pacing back and forth. Then he paused in front of Isaiah and looked him straight in the eye. "You proved you were just what Tony and Bucky called you, Isaiah. *Chicken! Chicken* because you didn't have enough guts to say, '*No! Not me!* I'm not going to get in trouble. Why should I steal a truck? I can think for myself!'

"You proved you were chicken, all right. Didn't you?" he demanded, pushing Isaiah down into the chair beside the desk. "You caved in to Tony and Bucky, and that very fact proves you were chicken."

Isaiah nodded his head in agreement. "Yes, Chip, I guess it does. I never thought about it that way. But, Chip! I know this sounds like an excuse, but I knew you wanted Tony to go to the game; and when I tried to give him the tickets, he said that I had let him down ever since he got me the job at Grayson's and—"

"*He* got you the job?" Chip interrupted. "That's a good one!"

Isaiah shook his head, and it was obvious he was trying to choose the right words. "You don't understand, Chip. Tony was the number-one boss, and Bucky was the number-two boss. Tony always decided who got the jobs, the newspaper routes and other kinds of jobs, and he appointed me for the job with you here."

"All right, so Tony and Bucky let you get the job. That isn't important. Besides, I had that figured out a long time ago. Now where do these new characters fit into the picture? The ones they call Rip and Skids? Somehow I don't think those are their given names."

Isaiah lowered his eyes, and Chip pressed the advantage. "They're running the corner now, aren't they? Haven't they taken over from Tony and Bucky?" Chip questioned, knowing the answer.

Isaiah nodded. "Yes," he managed in a low voice. Then, gathering confidence, he continued. "Yes, Chip, they have, but why shouldn't they? They're even older than you are! Just as big too!"

"Taking the truck was their idea, too, wasn't it?"

Isaiah was silent for a moment, and then the words came with a rush. He told about the arrival of two new families in the neighborhood and the appearance of Rip and Skids on the corner the same evening. "They moved right across the street from us, Chip. And they're always hanging out on the front steps or down at the corner. And they've got Tony and Bucky right where they want them. Bucky more than Tony though."

"What about the truck? What did they want you to do with it?"

"I wasn't supposed to do anything with the truck, Chip. Rip and Skids said it was a test for Tony and Bucky. Anyway, that's what Tony told me."

"What kind of test?"

"I don't know."

"But where were they taking the truck?"

"Tony never told me exactly, Chip. He said something about leaving the truck in an alley and that Rip and Skids would do the rest."

"Were they going to bring it back?"

"I don't know, Chip."

"I still don't understand why *you* thought you had to go."

"I told you, Chip. Tony and Bucky followed me and caught up with me after I left the store. Tony said he wanted me to come because I had to prove my loyalty to him just like he and Bucky had to prove their loyalty to Rip and Skids."

Chip shook his head. "That's a fine definition of loyalty," he said in disgust. "How in the world could Rip and Skids take the leadership away from Tony and Bucky so quickly and dominate them so easily?"

"Like I said before, Chip, they're *old!* Besides, Rip is a boxer, or used to be, and Skids is nearly as tough. And they don't mess around. You tell them you won't do something, and you get beat up! Period! They're not afraid of men either. They've already beat up a couple. For no reason at all, as far as I could see."

That was too much for Chip. He was bewildered. "But didn't the men report them to the police? Why didn't someone tell Pop King? Wouldn't he do something about it if he knew they were beating up everyone in sight?"

"Sure," Isaiah said significantly. "If he *knew* it, he might. But who's gonna tell him? Not *me!* I'm at least that smart!"

Chip conceded that point and was about to resume his pacing when Soapy interrupted, barging unceremoniously through the door. "C'mon, you guys," he urged. "We gotta get over to the Y for the tae kwon do competition." He appraised Isaiah. "How you feelin', champ?"

"He's all right," Chip said shortly. "You two go ahead. I've got to see Coach Ralston. Good luck, Isaiah. I hope you win."

Soapy's cheerful expression vanished. "Aw, no, Chip," he pleaded. "Aw, no!"

But Soapy was talking to himself. Chip was gone, threading his way up Main Street through the frenzied football crowd, before Soapy could say "curfew."

CHAPTER 15

Yellow-Belt Champion

COACH CURLY RALSTON was deeply absorbed in a last-minute review of the Dukes scouting notes. Chip paused at the door and waited, but Ralston was so deep in thought that it was several seconds before the big man sensed someone was there. When he saw Chip, he whipped his feet off the desk and swung upright like the recoil of a steel spring. "Hello, Chip," he said warmly, "you're early."

"I don't think so, sir. I guess that I'm just the opposite. At least I was last night."

"What do you mean?"

"I broke the curfew rule, sir. I was out after eleven o'clock."

Ralston stared at Chip in disbelief. "I don't understand," he said slowly. "Say that again."

Chip explained that he had gone on a personal errand after work and had been unable to get back to Jeff until nearly midnight. "I'm sorry, Coach," he said simply.

Ralston was caught by surprise. He chewed his underlip and regarded Chip speculatively. He was trying to determine a course of action. He leaned back in his chair and laced his hands behind his head. "I thought George Grayson lets his football players off early."

"He does, Coach."

"Wasn't it possible for you to take care of this business at some other time?"

"No, sir."

"I see." Ralston studied Chip briefly and then continued. "Is that all? Don't you have anything to add to what you've told me?"

"No, sir," Chip said, "except that it was something personal that couldn't wait, and I'm sorry."

Ralston nodded. "I believe that," he said. "All right, Hilton, I'll think it over. Thanks for telling me yourself before someone beat you to it."

Chip paused at the door. "Should I dress for the game, Coach?"

Ralston deliberated a long second. "Yes," he said at last, "you can suit up."

Chip retraced his steps and was back at Grayson's at 11:30. It had been a short talk and a fast trip, but a lot of ground had been covered. And he'd done the right thing.

Soapy and Isaiah returned from the Y shortly after twelve o'clock, the irrepressible redhead broadcasting to anybody who would listen that he was in distinguished company. "This, ladies and gentlemen," he cried, waving a hand grandiloquently toward Isaiah Redding, "is the newly crowned yellow belt—soon to be orange belt—tae kwon do champion of University, the state, undoubtedly the country, and, possibly, the universe."

Isaiah was as proud as an Olympic gold medalist. "I did it, Chip," he cried, "I did it! I beat everybody in forms, one-steps, breaking, and free-sparring!"

Soapy's exuberance evaporated as soon as he caught a glimpse of Chip's face. "Bad news?" he asked fearfully.

"I don't know," Chip said. "Come on, let's go."

Outside, Fireball, Whitty, and Biggie Cohen were surrounded by an admiring group. The fans opened up a path and shouted their encouragement as Chip and Soapy joined their teammates to walk to University Stadium.

"Go get 'em, Hilton!"

"Let's go, Smith!"

"How ya feelin', Biggie?"

"Pull in those passes, Whitty."

"Run one back for me, Fireball!"

In the locker room, Soapy edged over beside Chip. "What did Coach Ralston say?"

"Nothing. I told him I had broken the curfew rule and asked him if I should suit up and he said yes."

"Did you tell him about me?"

"No, Soapy, I didn't. You—"

Before Chip could finish the sentence, Soapy had turned and was on his way, striding purposefully out of the room. A few minutes later he was back, his lips set in a thin, tight line, the freckles standing out brown and clear through the unusual paleness of his complexion. "That's that!" he whispered grimly.

Nothing happened then or in the warm-up drills in the stadium. But when they left the field and gathered in the locker room for Ralston's last-minute instructions, the entire squad got a shock.

"You'll be playing this game without the services of two of your teammates today," Ralston said sharply.

"Chip Hilton and Soapy Smith have been benched for failure to observe the eleven o'clock curfew."

A dead, uncomfortable silence followed Ralston's words. And that silence seemed to drain all the fight and hustle out of the State team right there in the locker room. Ralston sensed what had happened to his team as soon as he finished the sentence; but it was done, and he was wise enough to realize that further discussion would not help the situation.

Nothing else helped State's football fortunes that afternoon. The players were sluggish on the defense, and Ralston's complicated offense fell flat without the wizardry of Chip's ballhandling. Burk did his best, but the spark just wasn't there. Fortunately, the opponents had a bad afternoon, too, fumbling just when their ground attack was eating up the first downs and a score seemed imminent, or running into a State interception the few times they ventured into the air. What had promised to be a brilliant battle between two football powers degenerated into a sluggish, uninteresting match.

Watching the Dukes' powerful running attack, Chip remembered Sullivan's scouting analysis. The Dukes followed the coach's description to the letter. They concentrated on basic football, staying with a bone-crushing, head-on ground contest, and they made State play their game.

Chip had been so wrapped up in his own misery that he had forgotten to look for Isaiah and Mark until the end of the first quarter. When he turned to look, Mark saw him and waved and yelled. Chip returned the greeting and was surprised to see Tony Carlara sitting between Isaiah and Mark.

And right then, right when the crowd noise stilled, a fan with a foghorn voice began to advise Ralston how to run the team.

"What you savin' Hilton for, Coach, the press conference?"

"C'mon, Ralston! Put number 44 in the game!"

Other fans in the vicinity of the head coach chimed in, and they raised a chant behind the State bench. When time was in and the teams were ready to play, the chant had spread and gathered momentum until it was a roar.

"We want Hilton! We want Hilton! We want Hilton!"

The action on the field caught the spectators' attention then, and the chant gradually died away. But it came right back when Burk tossed an interception. And it held straight through to the end of the scoreless half when the teams left the field.

Chip trailed along the sideline with a windbreaker covering the big 44 on his back. He was trying to be as inconspicuous as possible. But the fans knew him and recognized him, and they hurled questions at him all the way to the runway leading under the stadium.

Ralston caught it too. But if he heard the caustic criticisms, his posture didn't show it. He walked confidently along beside Rockwell, discussing the play of the first half as if he were in his own living room.

Chip had never felt so uncomfortable in his life. His teammates didn't say anything, but a wall of restraint was present. He sat down on the hard bench in the locker room under the stadium, thankful for trainer Murph Kelly's no-talking rule. After the players had rested and been checked by Murphy and his assistants, Ralston reviewed the first half. He quickly referred to the mistakes, mapped the second-half strategy, and finished by expressing his confidence in their ability to keep fighting. That was it, and when the second-half starters raced out on the field, Burk was still in at quarterback.

Walking back along the sideline to the bench with

Soapy, Chip again waved to Mark and Isaiah and checked out the occupants of his other seats. He recognized none of the corner crowd he knew, with the exception of Bucky Husta, who was sitting between two older guys he figured were the infamous Rip and Skids. All three were watching him intently.

Chip caught the eye of the fellow on Husta's left. The one wearing the open collar showing gold chains gestured toward him and shouted mockingly, "Where's the social worker, Coach? Put in the hero! Put in Hilton!"

Soapy heard the raucous voice and pulled back as if he was caught from behind. "Why, you—" he began.

Chip pulled Soapy forward. "Never mind," he said. "Don't pay any attention to him. You know you can't play this game with rabbit ears. Soapy, you hear too much."

Soapy was still glaring angrily at the stranger. "Who's the wise guy?" he asked fiercely. "Hey, he's in one of your seats!"

"It's not important," Chip said.

"That's gratitude!" Soapy raged. "You give 'em free tickets, and they make moronic comments behind your back."

"It's not important," Chip repeated. "Forget *them!* Can you see where Tony is sitting? That's what I'm interested in."

During the halftime intermission, the rival bands had entertained the fans with formations and music. But most of the State fans spent the interim trying to find out what was wrong with Chip Hilton. The sportswriters and the announcers were as much in the dark as the fans. They had unsuccessfully quizzed the State assistant coaches and were left to vague speculations. One reporter had approached Ralston on the field and was politely escorted from the sidelines.

FOURTH DOWN SHOWDOWN

FOURTH DOWN SHOWDOWN

Gee-Gee Gray had been a Hilton booster from the very first day he had seen him in action as a freshman. Now, up in the broadcasting booth, he was beside himself trying to explain why Chip was out of action. "We still don't know what's wrong with number 44, Hilton. *If* anything—

"Could be this is one of Curly Ralston's tricks. Could be he's holding his all-America candidate until State is in a scoring position. Now I'm second-guessing one of the greatest coaches in the business. Hmmm.

"Well, since I've taken over the State coaching job, I might as well go all out and try third-guessing. Hilton's a pretty valuable piece of football material, right? Now, suppose Ralston figured the Dukes are rough on passers, and since the game has no bearing on the conference championship, he might be holding Hilton out to avoid an injury! You don't go for that! Hmmm. Me either.

"It's not like Coach Ralston! It's not like Chip Hilton! That kid can take care of himself in any company.

"Now this is the last try. Honest! Hilton could have a pulled muscle or a sprained ankle. Could be . . .

"The teams are back on the field now, and State will kick off. I hope the fans here this afternoon brought their umbrellas and raincoats. The skies have turned dark and there's a rumble of thunder in the distance. The wind has really kicked up. We'll see if it becomes a factor.

"Ralston's starting his seven blocks of granite on the line, the Super Seven! Whittemore and Higgins at the ends! Cohen and Maxim, tackles! Two seniors in the guard spots, McCarthy and Clark. And the old, reliable Captain Mike Brennan at center.

"In the backfield, Ralston is starting the same foursome he sent out on the field for the first half: Morris, Finley, Gibbons, and Burk. Ace Gibbons will kick for State.

There's no score here in University Stadium at University in the game between State and the Grantland Dukes.

"Gibbons boots a high one! It's down to Jones on the Dukes' twenty-yard line. He's up to the twenty-five, the thirty, and he's downed by Tiny Tim McCarthy on the thirty-two-yard line.

"Here comes a reverse by Kytes, and he's really moving, but he'll go nowhere. Biggie Cohen has him cornered. Ouch! What a tackle! Wait a minute, there's a flag on the play.

"While we wait for the officials to sort this one out, here's a weather update from the University Meteorological Society: There is a severe storm watch in effect for the University area for the next three hours. Severe lightning and high winds have been reported in the adjoining county. There is the potential for flooding in low-lying areas. Stay tuned for future updates and be prepared to take action. This is Gee-Gee Gray for WSUN radio, home of the University Statesmen.

"Here we go. It's a penalty against State. It's an automatic first and ten at the spot of the foul. That places the ball on the Dukes' forty-six.

"Reed carries. First down! Reed got eleven yards on the play. That moves the ball down to the State forty-three-yard line. It will be first and ten! Kytes is at right half, Reed at quarterback, Jones at fullback, and Wheat at left halfback.

"Jones has the ball. He's racing through left tackle. Oops, there's a flag on the play. The Dukes' backfield was in motion. Captain Mike Brennan accepts the penalty, so it's first and fifteen for the Dukes on the State forty-eight. Brennan would probably have declined the penalty so the down would count, but Jones had carried the ball clear down to the State thirty-five-yard line.

"Here's another weather update from the University Meteorological Society: The severe weather front is approaching the University area. The severe weather watch has been updated to a warning. All residents in the University area are advised to stay tuned for updates as they develop."

Gee-Gee Gray's broadcast the rest of the afternoon was strictly an unvarnished word picture of a dull, uninteresting game that was still scoreless after four quarters of regulation play. The game officials declared the contest a tie since the overtime procedures couldn't be completed because of the weather.

Gray did say just before the game went off the air that Curly Ralston would be his guest on his seven o'clock sports roundup show and that he was sure the Chip Hilton story would be clarified at that time.

There was no celebrating after the game, although the fans could very well have accorded State that honor. Holding the mighty Dukes to a tie was no easy accomplishment.

Chip was tired and stiff from sitting the bench. And sitting it was, for there had been no action in the game exciting enough to bring him to his feet. He looked for Isaiah, Mark, and Tony when the game ended, but they were gone, lost in the crowd of hurrying fans filing out of the stands. Before he could move, it seemed, he was surrounded by reporters.

"What happened, Hilton? You hurt?"

"How come you didn't play?"

"What's the matter with *you,* Smith?"

A photographer came pushing through, adjusting his camera. "Hold it, guys. I've got to have a picture."

Soapy moved back for the picture, but Chip stopped

him. "I think you'd better ask Coach," he said. "Come on, Soapy. We've got to go." That worked with the photographer but not with the sportswriters. They pressed around Chip and Soapy in a solid ring, backed up now by fans who had reached the field. "Why didn't you play?" they demanded. "How come you sat the bench?"

Chip had never been in such a spot. He didn't know what to do or say, and, after the photographer incident, Soapy wasn't talking to anyone. Henry Rockwell saved the day. Rock didn't know why Chip had broken curfew, but he knew there had to be a good reason behind the infraction. He saw the milling group, nudged Ralston, and led the way through the crowd until he and the head coach were by Chip's side.

"Let's let the players get out of this weather. The coach will answer the questions," Rockwell said, addressing the reporters. He grasped Chip and Soapy each by an arm and gently started them toward the end of the field. "You two hit the showers and be quick about it."

Chip and Soapy trotted gratefully away, and Ralston answered the questions in the same dull voice that Gee-Gee Gray had broadcast the lackluster game. Hilton and Smith had been benched for breaking the eleven o'clock curfew. More drastic action other than today's benching would have been taken except they worked until 10:45 P.M.

"That doesn't give them much of a margin to get back to their dorm by eleven o'clock," Ralston explained, "and that's why they weren't suspended from the squad. They are reinstated as of now, and I expect to use them in the Midwestern game next Saturday. I might add that Hilton and Smith reported the matter themselves."

"And you want to be a sports reporter!" Soapy said scornfully as he and Chip made their way through the runway. "Why, they'd tear a guy to pieces to get a story!"

"They sure would," Chip agreed dourly.

Chip's teammates were in various stages of undressing when he and Soapy entered the locker room. There was no conversation except for a murmur of disgust and self-condemnation from the subdued players. Biggie, Whitty, Speed, Fireball, and Red Schwartz immediately surrounded them while other members of the squad merely looked up and as quickly looked away. Captain Mike Brennan was the exception, joining Chip's friends.

"What happened, Chip?" Brennan asked. "Tough break. We needed you out there this afternoon. Needed you and Smith both."

"We just couldn't make it home before eleven o'clock last night," Chip said. "We're sorry, Mike. We're sorry we let you and the team down."

"Who reported you?" Ace Gibbons demanded, joining Brennan. "It was a dirty thing to do!"

"No one reported us, Ace," Chip said quietly. "We told Coach ourselves."

Tiny Tim McCarthy closed his locker with a bang. "You'd think he'd have given you a break," he growled, "knowing you work every night! I don't see how you do it. Classes and studying and football and working! It's not—"

Tiny Tim cut off the words as if he had bitten his tongue and gestured toward the door. Curly Ralston and Henry Rockwell were standing there, waiting quietly. The two coaches hesitated a second and then advanced to the center of the locker room.

"That's all right, Tim," Ralston said gently. "I heard what you were saying and I agree to a point. However, Hilton and Smith *did* break the rule, and that left me no alternative." He paused and looked at Chip and Soapy. "Particularly, when they would give no explanation!"

CHAPTER 16

Soapy Makes the Sports Pages

STATE UNIVERSITY'S football fans had expected to win the game against the Grantland Dukes, and their confidence had been rudely shaken. But their loyalty was sure and strong, and the general philosophy heard all over University was expressed by Tims Lansing that evening when he dropped in to see Chip. "Hi ya, Chip," he said cheerfully. "You can't win 'em all!"

"I wish the guys could have won this one," Chip said. "Especially since—"

"I know," Lansing interrupted. "I heard the coach on Gray's sports broadcast. He's a great guy. He said the guys put up a solid fight and he was proud of their performance.

"I've been thinking about the field-goal reputation you've acquired, Chip. You know, every team you play realizes you're Mister Toe whenever State gets inside their forty-yard line.

"Now, wouldn't it be a good idea to work up a fake-kick play when you need six or seven points instead of three?"

"Sounds good," Chip agreed.

Lansing eyed Chip keenly as he pulled a piece of paper out of his pocket. "Thought you would say that, so I worked up a little play on my own. It's a perfect takeoff for the placekick formation the coach has been using." He spread the paper on the desk. "What do you think of it?"

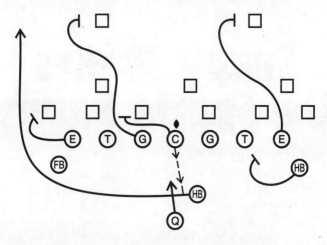

Chip scanned the outline. "It looks fine," he said. "I like it."

Lansing beamed. "It is good. You know why? Because Morris is fast and runs well to the left. Another thing, every team in the conference lines up in a 6-3-2 defense formation when they expect a placekick. And all of them play their linebackers up close, and that makes the blocking easier for a wide-end sweep. Right?"

"Right!" Chip echoed.

Lansing grinned with satisfaction and continued. "The pass is to Morris naturally, and you do just as always: take your step and kick. Only the ball isn't there.

SOAPY MAKES THE SPORTS PAGES

Morris has it, and he's running around left end. Morris has to be sure to have his knee off the ground when he catches the ball, and when you kick through his arms, he's got to hold the ball in his left hand. All right?"

Chip nodded. "It sure is. Mind if I keep the paper? You might be seeing this in a game before the season is over."

"Be sure to give me credit for an assist," Lansing joked. "Well, Chip, I gotta get to the library. See you Monday."

Soapy went through his human alarm clock routine the next morning, but much of his usual Sunday morning exuberance was missing. He pounded on the doors and handed out the papers, but then he hurried back to his room and crawled into bed. "First time this year I've had my name in the sports pages, and I don't want people to see it," he said gloomily. "Read Bill Bell's column."

Chip opened the *Herald* to the sports page and read Bell's story of the game.

STATE AND DUKES BATTLE TO SCORELESS TIE
State Misses Star Field General
by Bill Bell

State and the Dukes concentrated on old-fashioned football yesterday afternoon and proved the old adage of the irresistible force and the immovable object. The sixty minutes of straight football was not appealing to the 58,756 fans and students who packed the stadium, but it was an exhibition of line play at its best.

Both forward walls were superb in their offensive and defensive play.

State played without Chip Hilton, sensational sophomore quarterback, who was benched by Coach Curly Ralston for a violation of training rules. A teammate, Soapy Smith, was benched for the same reason.

The inclement weather forced game officials to terminate play during the overtime period. No resumption of play is expected since the game was a nonconference contest.

"It's not as bad as I thought it would be," Chip said.

Soapy grunted. "Read Locke's story in the *News*," he said shortly, waiting for Chip's reaction.

Chip found Locke's story without much difficulty. In fact, it practically jumped out of the sports page at him.

STATE AND DUKES TIE
HILTON BENCHED, TEAM DEMORALIZED
Fumbles Disastrous to Dukes
by Jim Locke

The Grantland Dukes were in a gratuitous mood yesterday afternoon in University Stadium. They fumbled conveniently and often, and if the locals had been playing any kind of football, their record this morning would not be marred by a tie.

Coach Curly Ralston benched quarterback Chip Hilton for a training violation just prior to the game, and this abrupt decision completely demoralized the State squad. Hilton would make no statement, but Ralston told the press that the star quarterback had been penalized for breaking a curfew regulation.

Thousands of State fans, myself included, are wondering just whom Ralston punished by benching

Hilton. It would seem that the penalty was directed more toward State than toward Hilton.

Ralston's poor timing undoubtedly upset his team and rendered it incapable of taking advantage of the numerous breaks Grantland served up all afternoon.

Although the game had no bearing on the conference standings, it further solidified my opinion that Ralston's sophomore team is beginning to come apart at the seams, and that further daydreams or nightmares about winning the conference championship had better be discarded.

Only the weather saved the Statesmen from a loss.

"Well?" Soapy demanded. Chip dropped the paper.

Chip shook his head and pressed his lips together in a grim line. "That's not fair to Coach. Locke practically blames him for not winning the game. Why didn't he criticize me? It was my fault. Guess I'll go downstairs and study. Coming?"

"You crazy? Not me! This is my day for hibernating!"

After church and lunch, Chip took a long nap and then spent the rest of the afternoon and evening studying. His friends tried to coax him to go out, but Chip had his work organized and stuck with it until ten o'clock. E-mails and Sunday night phone calls were postponed as he went to bed, his heart still heavy with thoughts of the game.

Ralston and his assistants poured it on Monday afternoon. The tie with the Dukes had no bearing on the conference standing, but it had been a shock. Now they were determined there would be no letdown in preparing for tough Midwestern, unpredictable Wesleyan, and mighty A & M. There was no bitterness or disappointment apparent from the members of the coaching staff, but each one, from Ralston down, was dead serious about his work. Chip was dead serious too. He couldn't help feeling self-conscious about being benched, although none of his teammates indicated in any way that they held him responsible for the tie game.

That evening, Herb Miller, the physical director at the Y, dropped by and asked Chip if he would participate in a little boxing program at the Y on Thursday night. "Isaiah is on the program for tae kwon do," he said, shaking hands with Chip's assistant, "and it's our big event of the season. If you could take part, it would go over big with the kids! Isaiah tells me you're pretty nifty with the gloves, and if you and I could put on a three-round exhibition, it would bring down the house. What do you say? There won't be anything to it as far as the boxing is concerned. It will be more fun than anything else."

"I haven't boxed since I was in high school," Chip protested. "You'd kill me! Besides, I don't think Coach Ralston would like it."

"He said it would be all right," Miller said quickly. "He just wanted to be sure you would wear headgear and that we would use twelve-ounce gloves. I haven't boxed three rounds for years. One thing is for sure, you're in better condition than I am. If I had to run the length of a football field just once, I'd keel over. I also spoke to Mr. Grayson, and he thought it was a great idea. He's on the Y board, you know."

"Well, I guess it would be OK," Chip consented, feeling pressured.

Chip was there Thursday night, and so was Frank Caruso with another man about his age and size. Isaiah, Mark, Tony, Bucky, and practically every kid from the Tenth Street corner were also in the bleachers. The whole neighborhood cheered when the yellow belts took their positions on the mat with Isaiah Redding at the front, leading the group through Basic 1 and Basic 2 forms for their tae kwon do demonstration.

Chip mentally kicked himself for having told Isaiah that he could box and for agreeing to appear on the program. But Isaiah was a wide-eyed witness, and Chip had given his word.

He sat in the rear of the crowd with the Y secretary. He was amazed at Isaiah's progress in the short time he had concentrated on the sport. Then Herb Miller came back and said it was time for them to get dressed.

Chip was recognized when he walked up through the crowd. The youngsters rose and applauded him. Those closest to the aisle jumped up for high-fives as he walked past. And when he climbed through the ropes and was introduced by the Y secretary, they stamped their feet and clapped until the man raised his hands for quiet. There wasn't much question about their admiration for State's varsity quarterback.

It really wasn't much of a boxing exhibition. Chip was in far better condition than Herb Miller and at the end of the third round had the instructor out on his feet. Miller grinned in appreciation when it was over and threw one arm over his rival's shoulder and raised Chip's other arm and hand in the air. "The winner," he cried, "and still champion!"

Frank Caruso and his friend, along with Mark and Isaiah, waited for Chip in the lobby. The pizzeria owner introduced Tony's father. "This is Tony's dad," he said. "Mr. Chip, meet Mr. Tony Carlara Sr."

Mr. Carlara greeted Chip warmly, gripping his hand and smiling. "I'm very glad to meet you, Mr. Chip."

"My name is Chip Hilton, Mr. Carlara. I know your son."

The little man smiled. "You know my Tony? That's good. Maybe you'll come visit my house sometime."

"I'd be glad to come. Well, excuse me, Mr. Carlara, Mr. Caruso. Isaiah and I have to hustle back to work. You going with us, Mark?"

Mark nodded, and they hurried back to Grayson's and back to the stockroom. Soapy was right behind them, carrying two shakes, his words flying. "How'd you make out, Isaiah, Chip? Ya beat 'em, huh? Atta boy! I knew you would! Drink this, champ! What are you doing here, Mark? Drink that and get going! You got school tomorrow. You, too, Isaiah."

Mark nodded, but he made no effort to leave. He looked from Chip to Isaiah and covertly rolled his eyes toward the door. Soapy got it and reacted as if he was pulling out of the line to run interference on an end run. "You want a Coke, Chip? I'll send it back with Isaiah. C'mon, Isaiah, I need your help."

As soon as the door closed behind them, Chip turned to the younger Redding. "What's up, Mark?"

"Isaiah's in for it with Rip and Skids, Chip. Guess they think he snitched about the truck. Anyway, they said he worked with you and that was the only way you *could've* known. They said a lot of other things, Chip. They said you wouldn't get away with it the next time."

"What did they mean?"

"I guess they meant you going down there and catching Tony and Bucky and Isaiah. I guess they meant they'd beat you up! That's what they do to everybody else."

CHAPTER 17

Crisis and Showdown

GEORGE GRAYSON was a quiet and unobtrusive man, but he was always available when friends needed help. The longtime owner of Grayson's and his wife had raised a house full of children. Now they were all married and living in various parts of the country. George and Jan Grayson missed them. Their children's visits back home never seemed long enough or often enough for the Graysons. His friends thought that was the main reason he helped so many young adults through school. The friendly man made it possible for his employees to go to college by arranging their hours around their class schedules and activities.

Those who knew the Graysons best knew the real reason. George remembered his own college days, when he had to struggle through day after day of hard work and study to earn his education. Ingrained in him was the belief that those times formed the foundation for his life. He credited his enriched life with his faith, family, business, and community to the lessons he learned through those tough, yet rewarding, times. Now, he hoped to provide opportunities for others to build their own foundations.

Narrowminded skeptics and jealous competitors said it was because he wanted to cash in on the business and publicity that athletes like Chip Hilton, Fireball Finley, Philip Whittemore, and Soapy Smith brought to Grayson's.

Whatever his reasons, there was no doubt about his enthusiasm for football. Friday he drove his football employees to University Stadium to reach their team buses for the short ride to the airport, where they would catch their early-afternoon flight to the all-important conference battle with Midwestern University.

A routine Friday at the airport turned into controlled mayhem when fans turned out to give a roaring send-off to the nearly one hundred athletes and their coaches, trainers, and managers who descended on the check-in counters for their charter flight to Midwestern. There was the usual excitement and banter that is present on any game trip, but flying added an elevated dimension to being a State varsity athlete. Curly Ralston was a stickler about his team's appearance and decorum. Every State coach, player, and manager proudly wore the school colors—a blue blazer, white shirt, blue-and-red tie, and khaki slacks.

Under Ralston's program, everyone knew the established boarding and seating order: university administrators and their guests first; next, coaches, followed by trainers; then senior, junior, and sophomore players; and last, the student managers and student trainers.

As sophomores, the Hilton A. C. members were near the back of the line as the team boarded the plane. "Chip,

I don't think there's enough room for all of us," Soapy fretted.

Red Schwartz couldn't resist tormenting Soapy as they filed past the administrators and coaches, "Don't worry, Soapy, there's enough seats." Then Red lowered his voice to a whisper. "But I did overhear the flight attendants say they were worried about having enough meals and beverage service for those in the back of the plane. Glad I ate a big breakfast. How 'bout you, Soapy?"

Soapy whipped his head around. "What? No! They can't! They have to have enough! Look, those administrators and the coaches already have juice and a goodie. That does it! From now on Soapy Smith flies first class!"

A hamlike hand grasped Soapy's shoulder. "Come on, Soapy, stop looking and get moving before we find room for you in the overhead," Biggie drawled.

Midwestern University was playing before a homecoming crowd, and the players were determined and full of fight. It was a tough game, a battle of two strong defensive teams. Midwestern kicked to Speed, and he brought the ball back to the thirty-yard line. Chip started at quarterback and tested the home team's pass defense on the first down, hiding the ball with fakes and flipping a quick buttonhook to Larry Higgins that was good for seven yards.

"Zone pass defense," Chip reported in the huddle. "We'll use our Z passes until they change. Now let's try forty-six on a count of three!"

Fireball drove straight ahead over center, and Chip faked to give him the ball. Chip faked again to Speed cutting toward the right flat, pivoted left, and aimed the ball toward Whittemore darting downfield near the left sideline. Then he twisted back and fired a hard pass to Speed far out in the right flat. It was a zone, all right. The defender hit Speed as soon as he caught the ball. Chip noticed that the middle linebacker trailed along the line of scrimmage.

Chip glanced quickly at the middle zone. The defense had shifted to the right with the middle guard filling the hole. "Good defense," he muttered. "Tough!"

And tough it was! Both teams played a tight defense. Midwestern scored twice in the first half and kicked both extra points. State tallied on a touchdown, and Chip kicked the extra point. The score at the end of the half was Midwestern 14, State 7.

State came back fighting in the second half, holding Midwestern for no gain on the twenty after Chip kicked the ball into the end zone. Midwestern had to punt, and Speed took the hard-drilling spiral on State's forty-five-yard line and carried for ten to the home team's forty-five. Then State marched on the ground to the twelve, where the Midwestern line stiffened and held. On third down, ten to go, Chip sent Fireball wide around right end. The hard-charging back was forced toward the sideline, and for a moment it looked as if he would be thrown for a big loss. At the last instant, he spotted Speed standing all alone in the far corner of the end zone. Finley fired a desperate, wobbly pass. Speed didn't miss the catch, and Chip didn't miss the extra point. That tied up the score at 14-14.

The two teams battled furiously and evenly in the fourth quarter, the ball changing hands half a dozen times. Chip's long, high punts gradually began to tell, and as the clock ran out, State had the ball on the Midwestern fifteen-yard line, fourth down and eight to go. Every fan in the stadium knew what was coming, and the old familiar "Block that kick! Block that kick! Block that kick!" chant came sweeping down on the players from all sides. Chip and Speed collaborated perfectly on the kick, and the ball sailed end over end and straight through the middle of the uprights. State had won its sixth-straight conference game, 17-14.

An away victory—particularly a *big* and especially pleasing victory—makes a great traveling companion. As the Statesmen boarded the plane for their return flight, the mood was upbeat, the volume was loud, and the banter among teammates was playful. As the plane leveled off, players settled down with their Walkmans, watched the inflight programs, or grabbed a nap. Chip, Soapy, Speed, Biggie, Whitty, Fireball, and Red had managed to grab a group of seats together and were discussing Tims Lansing's play. "It will work in the right spot," Fireball said. "It's simple enough."

"Yes, but the other team would have to think we were going to kick the field goal for sure," Speed said. "That means everyone would have to do a good job in faking their blocks, or I'd end up in the bleachers."

"What's this?" a familiar voice boomed. "Someone trying to steal my job?"

Chip knew that voice. He had sensed Coach Ralston's presence when his friends quieted so suddenly. He looked up and grinned. "They would have to be awfully good," he said, rising to his feet.

"Sit down, sit down," Ralston said. "Now, what's the play?"

"It's a play Tims Lansing worked up, Coach," Chip explained. "He figured it might work when the other team was expecting us to kick a field goal."

He handed the piece of paper to Ralston and continued. "It's a whole lot like our K 77, sir, except in that play the kicker actually kicks. It's up to Speed or whoever is holding the ball to pull it back at the last second." He studied Ralston's reaction. "What do you think, Coach?"

"Not bad," Ralston said, studying the paper. "Not bad at all. I think I'd make one or two little changes though. Make it a little tougher on the kicker. I'd let him run through the ball, all right, but then I'd have him chase the secondary defender closest to our center and send the center down for the block on their defensive right back. Got a pencil, Rock?"

He sketched the play quickly on the back of Chip's paper. "Here, like this!" Ralston handed the paper back to Chip and waited. "What do you think? Any better?"

Chip nodded. "Much better."

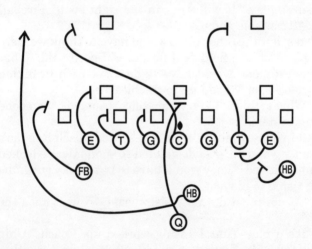

"Keep in mind," Ralston continued, "that the line would have to hold for at least a three-count before sliding left to get good blocking angles. Another thing. Speed has to keep his right hand and arm out straight and let you kick right through it. And he's got to keep the ball hidden with his left hand. Suppose you study it some." He glanced around the circle of faces and grinned. "Looks as if you've got about everyone who is in on the play right here. All but Mike Brennan. Right, Rock?"

Chip and his teammates talked over the play and then, gradually, one after the other, drifted off to sleep. It seemed only a few minutes until Soapy elbowed Chip and mimicked: "Chip, it's time to return all your carry-on items to the overhead compartments, stow your tray table in its locked position, and be sure your seat is in its upright position and your seat belt is securely fastened."

The groggy quarterback could only reply, "Carry-on what?"

"Wake-up," Soapy laughed. "We're getting ready to land."

Soapy shook Chip's shoulder and thrust a Sunday newspaper under his nose. "Something to think about," Soapy said, pointing to the headline.

A & M DEFEATS GRANTLAND 21-7, SIXTEENTH STRAIGHT
The Dukes' First Loss in Sixteen Games

A & M won its sixteenth-consecutive victory today, downing the nearly invincible Dukes for their first loss in sixteen games. A & M has now won nine straight this season, extending the Aggies' consecutive victory string to sixteen straight over a two-year period. The Aggies are idle now until the State game on Thanksgiving Day.

The Dukes were no match for the conference champions this afternoon. The Aggies ran through, around, and over them to win the much-touted battle of bowl champions. A & M has now scored a total of 295 points to their opponents' 41.

"How about our game?" Chip asked.

"Next page," Soapy said quickly. "Friend of mine made the headlines!"

STATE EDGES MIDWESTERN 17-14
ON HILTON'S KICKING

Mister Toe Boots Winning Field Goal
Locals Come from Behind to Win

State came from behind here today to win an important conference game over Midwestern, 17-14. It was a bitterly fought contest and was decided only because of the sensational kicking of Chip Hilton, State's excellent sophomore quarterback. Midwestern had the edge in the first half, scoring twice and kicking the extra points to lead State, 14-7.

But Chip Hilton, playing his first game in two weeks, proved that he is one of the finest quarterbacks in the country. He directed his team brilliantly to a 14-14 tie and then used his superior punting ability to pin Midwestern back in its own territory most of the final period. The margin of victory was a three-point field goal from the Midwestern fifteen-yard line by Hilton as the game ended.

State unquestionably looms as a serious contender for conference honors, despite the brilliant record of A & M. Wesleyan is the sole remaining obstacle that State must hurdle to qualify as a challenger to A & M leadership.

CRISIS AND SHOWDOWN

"One to go," Soapy observed as Chip finished the story. "We'll kill 'em!"

After church, Soapy headed back to Jeff for his Sunday afternoon snooze and Chip started down to Pete's Restaurant for lunch. Just as he turned the corner of Main and Tenth, he met Isaiah's aunt, Mrs. Clark. They chatted a few minutes about football and then talked about Isaiah and the neighborhood problems.

"Isaiah *is* a good boy, Chip. He is frail and weak physically—although I must say that you're doing wonders with him—but he has a fine mind and a wonderful attitude. Sometimes he acts more like the head of the family than his father. But he needs guiding. In fact, all the children in the neighborhood need that. They need leadership, leadership by someone they respect and admire, someone with ideals and ambitions.

"If my brother John would only assume more responsibility and spend more time with the boys, things would be different. I can handle the girls, but I think the boys need a man to help them. But John gets discouraged and he's not home a lot since he works so many hours to make ends meet. But here I am talking all about myself and my troubles when it's such a nice day. A young man like you should be enjoying himself. I hope you'll come to see us soon. Good-bye."

The State campus was buzzing about the conference championship the next week. Chip had become a campus hero, but he didn't like it. Perhaps that was too strong. He liked it, but he wished everybody wouldn't make such a big deal of it. Everything seemed to be going too smoothly, and he had a feeling it was too good to last.

Isaiah was his old self, smiling and cheerful. "Tony's my best friend now," he told Chip one evening. "You going to have the tickets this week?"

"I'll have the tickets, all right," Chip assured him. "Ten of them!"

Later that evening, Mark came in for his nightly milk shake and told Chip that Tony was a different kind of person. "He's been over at our house with Isaiah almost every night," he confided. "He and that Rip guy had some kind of an argument. Anyway, Tony doesn't hang around the corner anymore."

"How about Bucky?"

Mark wrinkled his nose. "Oh, he hangs around down on the corner with Rip and Skids all the time."

"Don't Rip and Skids work?"

"Nope. I heard them talking to the guys on the corner one night, and Rip was saying that only stupid guys work."

"Where do they get their money and clothes? They always seem to be wearing nice clothes. They look new."

Mark snorted. "Nice clothes? Yuck! You call that stuff they wear nice? You couldn't give me clothes like that! I think they look stupid!" Mark's loud straw noises and smacking lips signaled he'd hit the bottom. "Well," he said, "guess I'd better go home."

Chip visited with Frank Caruso several times that week and learned that he and Tony's father and some of the other men in the neighborhood were getting together so they could do something about the kids. At Chip's suggestion, Mr. Caruso promised to ask John Redding to join forces with them.

On Friday, Chip met Pop King in Pete's Restaurant for a sandwich. "Pop, do you know two guys called Rip and Skids?"

"Sure I know them, Chip. They grew up here in University. Just moved into this neighborhood. They used to live over on the north side. They've had a few run-ins with us but nothing serious. Rip used to be a club boxer of some sort. He's a tough youngster. Guess I shouldn't call him a youngster anymore though. Must be twenty-two at least."

"Isn't there any way you can keep them away from the kids?"

"No, but I'm watching 'em. They all hang out in the same place. I don't want them influencing the kids either."

"What are their real names?"

"Rip is Tommy Grasco and Skids is Joe Welks. I haven't figured out why they're so interested in hanging around with the kids on the corner, but I'll bet my badge it's for no good!"

That night, trouble was back. Isaiah was wearing his whipped-dog expression and had gone back in his shell. Mark came in later, and Chip sent Isaiah out with some syrups for the fountain.

"What's wrong with Isaiah, Mark?"

"I heard him crying last night after we went to bed. Rip, Skids, and Bucky slapped him around."

"What for?"

"Just caught him coming home from work. I guess it was something about him and Tony and not reporting or something like that."

"Reporting?"

"Well, it's the same with Tony. He stopped hanging around the corner, and they had a showdown with him and said they'd make him a lieutenant or something. Looks like they got Tony scared, although he stood right up to them. Anyway, Isaiah wouldn't join or report, whatever they call it, and they beat him up.

"They boss the whole neighborhood now. They're nothing but bullies, but I'm getting tougher. Feel my arm!"

Isaiah came back then and quietly did his work. But Chip noticed that Isaiah gave Mark one of those you-didn't-tell-him-did-you? looks. A few minutes later Mark said good night and left for home. When it was time for Isaiah to leave, Chip gave him the tickets for the game and was surprised by his sudden reluctance to accept them.

"What's the matter, Isaiah? Are you in trouble again?"

"No, Chip, I'm fine. I'm just tired, I guess."

"You look tired. You go on home and get a good night's rest."

Isaiah's attitude disturbed Chip, and he made a quick decision. He closed and locked the stockroom door and told Mitzi he would be back in twenty minutes. Then he hurried out the Tenth Street door. He looked down Tenth Street, but Isaiah was not in sight. In fact, there wasn't a soul walking down Tenth. Chip glanced quickly toward Main and caught sight of Isaiah just as he turned the corner. Chip trailed him all the way down Main Street.

The neighborhood gradually changed, from businesses to homes and then to Isaiah's neighborhood. Up ahead, Isaiah hurried purposefully along, but then he turned to the right and vanished up an alley. Chip quickened his pace and entered the dark opening. Isaiah had stopped at his own street and was carefully peering around the corner.

Chip waited in the darkness. Then Isaiah suddenly streaked around the corner for home. Chip heard someone yell, and he sprinted forward. At the corner he paused and scanned the scene. Isaiah was racing toward his house in the middle of the block, and tearing down the street from the pizzeria corner were three shadowy figures. Isaiah sprang up the steps to his house and slammed the Redding front door almost in the faces of Bucky Husta, Rip Grasco, and Skids Welks.

Chip breathed a sigh of relief and turned back down the alley. Now the picture was clear. The crisis had arrived. The showdown could no longer be avoided or postponed.

CHAPTER 18

Makes a Football Talk

CHIP TRIED to put Isaiah's predicament out of mind when he went to bed later that night, but he just couldn't do it. He tossed and turned all night and started for Grayson's just as the sun peeked over the horizon. By the time Soapy, Fireball, Whitty, Mitzi, and the rest of the staff checked in, Chip's usual Saturday morning work was all finished. He waited impatiently for Isaiah to arrive. But nine o'clock passed and then ten and eleven and eleven-thirty, and still no Isaiah, and no Mark. Then the excitement of the game caught up with him, and he had to force himself to turn his thoughts away from the boys and on to football.

It was a beautiful football day: cool, crisp, and clear but with enough haze in the sky to eliminate the glare of the sun. The stands were nearly filled when State lined up to kick off to Wesleyan. And somewhere in the giant bowl, gossip had it, the entire A & M squad and coaching staff were there to make a firsthand appraisal of the Statesmen.

Chip looked over behind the bench and was surprised to see that his seats were filled with strangers. All except the three on the end. Bucky, Rip, and Skids were seated in these and appeared to be watching him intently. Then the game whistle shrilled, and Chip forgot everything except the ball sitting up on the tee, six short strides away.

The game progressed according to form. Wesleyan could not gain and punted to Speed and Fireball on the forty-yard line, and Speed carried the ball back to the visitors' forty. Then State scored in exactly four plays, and Chip kicked the extra point.

So at the end of the first three minutes of play, State led, 7-0. After Chip kicked the ball into the end zone, the State defense took over, giving Chip a chance to look for Isaiah and Mark from the sidelines. But they were not in sight, not in his seats nor anywhere behind them in the section. When State scored two more touchdowns in the first quarter, Ralston decided to give Chip a rest and brought in Burk to finish out the first half.

Chip got back in the game at the start of the second half, and as he ran out on the field, he heard the raucous voice he had associated with Rip Grasco yell something about "social worker!" He promised himself he would stay cool and ignore Rip's comments. But when the game was over, he would find out what happened to Isaiah and Mark. And he'd have a little talk about those tickets too.

The second half would have been a slaughter if Ralston had kept his starters in the game and given them free rein. But the wily mentor worked his squad under wraps, limiting the attack to straight on-the-ground football, and used his first string sparingly.

Chip started the third quarter, but Ralston pulled him right after the kickoff. He got his last chance in the final four minutes when Ralston sent him in to boot a field goal from the Wesleyan twenty-five-yard line. The kick was good and ended the scoring for both sides. The final score was State 40, Wesleyan 14.

As soon as the game ended, Chip sprinted off the field and over to the section behind the State bench. Rip, Skids, and Bucky were walking slowly away. Chip grabbed Bucky by the arm and swung him around. "Where's Isaiah?" he demanded.

Bucky was surprised and cowed for an instant. "How do I know?" he snarled, jerking away.

"Yeah, and what do we care?" Rip Grasco added nastily. He nudged Skids Welks as Chip faced him. "Looks almost tough with all that padding on, doesn't he, Skids?"

"Yeah," Skids agreed, "ain't that a joke?"

Chip ignored them and turned back to Bucky. "Where'd you get the ticket for that seat?" he demanded.

"None of your business," Bucky said boldly. "I got it, didn't I?"

"Yeah," Rip added, "he got it the same place I got mine. Want to make something out of it?"

Chip eyed Rip steadily, nodding his head. "Yes," he said calmly, "I do. It wouldn't be a bad idea at all. I'll see *you* later."

"Anytime, social worker," Rip sneered. "Anytime, anywhere!"

"Remember just that," Chip said. "Anytime, anywhere." He turned away and trotted for the runway. Now to find out what had happened to Isaiah and Mark.

The State locker room was in an uproar. But above the celebration, Chip could hear Soapy yelling, "Move over, Florida! Move over, Georgia! Move over, Nebraska! Move over, Oklahoma! You got company!"

Ralston and Rockwell smiled as they watched

MAKES A FOOTBALL TALK

Soapy's performance. Finally, Murph Kelly got the team quieted down long enough for the head coach to make an announcement. Ralston was grinning from ear to ear, and Chip got the impression it wouldn't take much for the head coach to shed his dignity and join in the fun.

"Nice going, men," he said gleefully. "You've come a long way since October second. Not that I ever doubted you could do it, once you realized your strength. I want to add the congratulations of the staff to all those you're going to receive tonight and tomorrow.

"Now, I don't want to throw cold water on your happiness, but I want to remind you, as I have so many times this season"—he paused and grinned briefly—"thank goodness one victory, or seven victories, does not make a season. We still have the big one to go, the one for the championship!

"There is no curfew tonight. But beginning tomorrow, Sunday, and continuing right through the week until we beat A & M on Thanksgiving Day, all training regulations, including a strict curfew check, are in effect.

"Thursday afternoon will come all too soon. We'll be leaving here Wednesday morning and will work out that afternoon on the A & M freshman field. A & M's athletic department has guaranteed us strict privacy for the practice sessions. That's all."

Grayson's was jammed that night with celebrants and customers. The entire crew was kept on the go. Isaiah didn't show up and neither did Mark, and Chip was worried. "I'll just go down there and find out what's wrong," he muttered. "Right after work!"

Then, at eight o'clock, Mark walked in with Soapy right behind him. Mark's face was scratched, and he had a cut lip and the beginning of a black eye.

"What happened to you?" Chip exclaimed.

Mark ignored the question. "Isaiah's sick," he said. "He had some trouble with Bucky." He explained that Isaiah had started to work that morning and Bucky was waiting for him. "They had a fight, Chip, and Isaiah got Bucky down and had him whipped until Skids pulled him off. Then Tony came running out of the house and jumped on Skids, and Rip took on Isaiah, and I just hit everybody.

"Then Rip and Skids took the football tickets away from Isaiah. It's been some day! Say, I heard we won!"

"Why didn't you call me or come in earlier tonight? I've been worried."

"Well, Pop's at work—he works from four o'clock to midnight—and Aunt Edith wouldn't let either one of us out of the house until she had to go shopping. So after she put the girls to sleep and told Isaiah to watch them, she took me with her to get the groceries. She's smart! She goes down to the markets when they're getting ready to close on Saturday nights, and that way she gets a lot of things cheap. Sometimes she gets things for nothing. I always help her carry them home," he said proudly. "I'm supposed to meet her in a few minutes at the market."

"Who gave you the black eye?" Soapy asked.

"Gee, I don't know. Guess I've got to learn some more of that tae kwon do. I didn't do so good."

"You got that right," Chip said dryly.

"The jerks!" Soapy exploded. "How long are we gonna let them get away with this?"

"Never mind," Chip said, motioning him toward the door. "You go back to work. I want to talk to Mark for a few minutes."

After Soapy left, Mark added, "They've got some kind of a meeting Tuesday night, Chip, and Isaiah's scared.

Rip and Skids said they had to go away for a couple of days; but when they get back, Isaiah is going to be disciplined. Pop will be at work, and I don't know what to do."

"Let me figure it out, Mark. What time are they going to have this meeting?"

"I guess it will be at night down in the alley. They always meet on the corner and then go down in the alley where Mr. Caruso keeps his truck. That's where they hang out when they're playin' cards or plannin' something."

"Isn't it pretty dark in the alley?"

"Oh, you can see all right. But they always hold court and settle the arguments there. Most of the time at night, so they can get away if Pop King tries to bust it up."

"I see," Chip said thoughtfully. "Now, Mark, I'll be studying at the dorm all day and working every evening. If Isaiah meets Rip or Skids or goes down to that alley any time, day or night, you call me. Understand? No matter what time it is, call me. Here's my number at Jeff. Now don't lose it and don't forget."

Mark straightened his square little shoulders. "I won't," he promised. "And, Chip, you won't tell Isaiah I snitched—I mean, you won't tell him I was here, will you?"

Chip shook his head. "No, I won't tell him. I won't tell him anything. Now you run along and meet your aunt."

The next morning, Soapy was back on the job as Jeff's Sunday newspaper carrier. "C'mon, Chipper," he said cheerfully, tramping about the room, "read all about it! Read all about the championship bout scheduled for Thanksgiving Day when the indefatigable, invincible, 'in-your-face-ables'—meaning State of course—and the fatigued, farinaceous farmers—long for Aggies—meet for the championship of all points north, south, east, and west, including the upside-down bowl! Read, oh, wonderful quarterback, read and smile!" He tossed the *Herald*, opened to the sports section, on Chip's bed.

STATE AND A & M MEET FOR
CONFERENCE CHAMPIONSHIP
Game of the Week to Be Televised
by Bill Bell

State and A & M meet for the conference championship Thursday afternoon in the game of the week, which will be nationally televised and watched by more than twenty-five million fans. The defending champion, A & M, is a strong favorite with practically every writer in the country. I would like to go on the record as a challenger of the consensus.

The defending champion, A & M, has a far better record. However, this is a game in which records and every other advantage, fact and fancy, go overboard when the teams line up to do battle.

This will be my forty-third game between these two rivals. Therefore, I predict State will be the team wearing the conference crown when the sun sets on the Aggie Stadium Thursday afternoon.

Not the least of the factors influencing my belief is the presence in the State lineup, and the good health, of State's "Mister Toe," Chip Hilton, who can do everything with a football except make it talk.

Chip tossed the paper on the floor. "Why does he do that?" he said irritably. "Every game! I don't see why the rest of the team doesn't get up a petition to stop the Hilton publicity! I'd sign it!"

"Maybe it's because they feel the same way," Soapy said. "You know something, Chipper? If the squad held a meeting to decide the most popular player on the team, you'd get every vote."

"Oh, stop it, Soapy," Chip said angrily. "You're as bad as Bill Bell! He doesn't know what he's writing about half the time. Why doesn't he write about the team? Teams win games, not individuals."

"He does," Soapy said. "Read on! Read it out loud."

Chip picked up the paper from the floor and continued, reading aloud.

Hilton runs like an Emmitt Smith, passes like a John Elway, handles the ball like another Houdini, blocks and tackles with the best of them, and can play sixty minutes of knock-'em-down and drag-'em-out football. But it's his kicking that gives State the edge. Hilton's punting average is one of the best in the country. And his deadly field goal accuracy will be a three-point threat every time State is stopped inside the Aggie thirty-yard line.

Further, this sports maven feels that in good old dependable Mike Brennan, Ace Gibbons, Tiny Tim McCarthy, and Larry Higgins, State has four veterans who could replace their respective A & M opponents with plenty to spare.

A & M is loaded with veterans, but the record proves that Curly Ralston knew what he was doing when he replaced last year's regulars and risked his reputation on seven newcomers: Biggie Cohen, Philip Whittemore, Soapy Smith, Joe Maxim, Speed Morris, Fireball Finley, and Chip Hilton.

"Now that's more like it," Chip crowed. "Hey! He picked you over Dex Clark! Shows he knows his football!"

"But you just said Bill Bell didn't kno—"

"Never mind! I take it back!"

"OK. Now read what Jim Locke says!"

STATE BURIES WESLEYAN, 40-14
Wesleyan No Match for Cocky Statesmen
by Jim Locke

State ran roughshod over a weak Wesleyan team here today to win its seventh-straight conference game. The Statesmen will meet A & M Thanksgiving Day in a bid for conference honors.

Both teams have played Grantland. State was blessed by the weather and lucky to escape with a scoreless tie, while A & M trounced Grantland on November 13 by a score of 21-7.

A & M did not play today and will be well rested for the game on Thursday. I've seen both teams in action and believe A & M will run State right out of the Aggie Stadium. The veteran Aggies pack too much experience for an overgrown bunch of freshmen and are headed for national honors with this conference championship.

Despite the presence of such stellar performers as Captain Mike Brennan, Ace Gibbons, Tiny Tim McCarthy, Dex Clark, and Larry Higgins, the game should end in a rout.

Curly Ralston has used his veterans sparingly this season with the exception of the five named above and has managed (with luck) to squeeze through a weak conference schedule to qualify for title consideration. The season schedules and results are shown below:

MAKES A FOOTBALL TALK

What Do You Think?

A & M			STATE		
30 -	Southwestern	13	24 -	Tech	21
28 -	Wesleyan	0	17 -	Brandon	14
51 -	Washington	0	31 -	Washington	6
28 -	Tech	2	29 -	Southwestern	27
33 -	Brandon	6	31 -	Cathedral	14
20 -	Midwestern	7	0 -	Grantland	0
39 -	Riordon	6	17 -	Midwestern	14
45 -	Cathedral	0	40 -	Wesleyan	14
21 -	Grantland	7			
295		41	189		110

"Likes us, doesn't he?" Chip said, smiling.

Soapy glowered. "'Overgrown bunch of freshmen,'" he growled. "Where does he get that nonsense?"

The redhead was restless and went for a walk shortly afterward, but Chip hit the books. Soapy came back after lunch and brought Chip two sandwiches and a carton of milk. Then, at two o'clock, Mark called Chip on the phone.

"Hi, Chip, this is Mark. We just finished delivering the papers. You know something? Bucky followed us this morning, the whole time. He told us Rip and Skids had assigned him to check up on Isaiah until they got back. Bucky said Rip and Skids would take it out on me if Isaiah didn't show up for the meeting Tuesday night."

"What's Isaiah going to do?"

"I don't know, Chip. But he wouldn't like it if he knew I called you."

"I won't tell him. But you be sure to call me if Isaiah ever goes down in that alley with Rip or Skids. OK?"

"Sure, Chip. Sure."

"All right. See ya later."

Classes were in full swing before the Thanksgiving holiday. Ralston called practice for two o'clock on Monday afternoon and kept the players at it until six o'clock. Isaiah showed up that evening still showing signs of his battle with Bucky Husta; but he was back in his shell, and so Chip said nothing about the game or the tickets. It was the same on Tuesday. Isaiah wouldn't speak except to answer direct questions, and Chip didn't press him.

Mark dropped in for his shake around seven o'clock and could barely conceal his excitement. Chip recognized the signs and sent Isaiah on an errand.

Mark started talking as soon as Isaiah was out the door. "Rip and Skids are back, Chip. They got back this afternoon, and Tony said they were going to hold the meeting tonight."

"Let them hold it," Chip said lightly. "I'm not interested unless Isaiah joins them. Here's a quarter. Will your aunt let you go out to use the pay phone?"

"If it's important she will, and this is important."

"Good. Now you go home and call me right away if Isaiah goes to that meeting. You remember our number at Jeff?"

Mark nodded. "I have it, Chip." He walked slowly to the door and hesitated. Then he turned. "Chip," he said in a low voice, "you know something? I'm kinda scared!"

CHAPTER 19

Under the Rock

ISAIAH REDDING raised himself cautiously on one elbow and looked intently at the bed on the other side of the room. Then, satisfied that his little brother was asleep, Isaiah slipped out of bed and quickly and silently pulled on his jeans and sweatshirt. Holding his shoes in one hand, he crept to the door, opened it a crack, and listened. Hearing no sounds in the house, he tiptoed down the stairs to the first floor and quietly slipped out the front door.

Upstairs, at the window overlooking the street, Mark watched Isaiah walk west toward the pizzeria. Then Mark pulled on his sweater and jeans, made sure the quarter was still in his pocket, and put on his sneakers. He moved down the steps like a shadow and disappeared east in the direction of Main Street.

Chip was just dozing off when the phone rang. Pouncing for the phone, he glanced at Soapy and then at their alarm clock. It was 11:30, and his roommate appeared sound asleep.

"You better hurry, Chip. Isaiah just went up the street."

"Where are you?"

"At the phone booth at the convenience store."

"All right. Now, pay attention. You go right home and stay there. I'll have Isaiah back there in no time. All right?"

"Right, Chip. But be careful."

Chip dressed quietly. Then he tiptoed out of the room, down the steps, and out the front door. His long legs carried him swiftly and silently along the quiet streets. As he ran, he tried to plan how he would get Isaiah and himself away from there. But everything was so uncertain that he decided he would have to react to the situation. He'd have to be ready for anything.

Soapy jumped out of bed as soon as Chip closed their door. Pulling on his clothes as he went from room to room, he quickly awakened Chip's friends and told them to get up and dress. "Meet me in my room," he whispered. "Right away!"

They were right behind him in various stages of dress and alertness. "Chip's in trouble," he said bluntly.

"What do you mean?" Biggie asked. "How do you know?"

"I just know," Soapy said. "Isaiah Redding is in trouble with some hoods, and Chip's gone to help."

"At this time of night?" a sleepy-eyed Whittemore said incredulously. "Why, it's almost midnight. I was having a great dream too."

"That's why I know it's real trouble," Soapy said shortly. "Chip wouldn't break curfew unless it was serious."

"You know where he went?" Biggie demanded.

"I've got a good idea."

"Well, what are we waiting for?" Fireball said, starting for the door. "If Chip's in trouble, I want to help! Who cares what time it is?"

Biggie Cohen suddenly filled the door. "Now wait a minute," he said quickly. "*I'll* go with Soapy, and the rest of you stay here and stay out of trouble. We won't need any help."

"Maybe not," Fireball said crisply, "but you're going to have it! If it comes to a choice between a curfew and helping Chip, I'm on my way!"

Whittemore nodded emphatically. "Me too!" he said. "Let's go!"

Red Schwartz suddenly erupted into action, dashing for the door and ducking under Biggie's heavy arm. "Hold it a minute," he cried over his shoulder. "I gotta get my shoes!"

Meanwhile, Chip had reached and ducked into the same doorway he and Mark had waited in the night of the incident with Mr. Caruso's truck. Chip saw the usual crowd on the corner. He could make out Isaiah and Tony and Rip and Skids, right in the middle of the group. Rip had Isaiah by the neck of his sweatshirt and was shaking him and yelling in his face. Tony was listening impassively, his arms folded across his chest.

Chip stepped boldly onto the sidewalk and started deliberately across the street. Isaiah was the first to see him and tried to push Rip's hand away. Rip turned then and saw the advancing figure. His grip ripped Isaiah's sweatshirt. Rip was shocked for a brief moment to see Chip but recovered his swaggering assurance when Skids moved beside him.

"Well, well," he mocked. "Look who's here! The social worker! Mr. College!"

Chip kept walking until he was right in front of Rip and Skids. "That's right," he said easily. "The social worker! I got to thinking about the tickets and what you said about making something out of it, and I figured this was as good a time as any."

"So what?" Rip sneered. "Go ahead! Make something out of it!"

The crowd of boys had pressed closely around Rip and Chip at first, but now they began to move back in awed silence, not really understanding what was happening to their "leader."

Chip saw Tony move closer to Skids, and Isaiah began to edge toward Bucky. This was getting out of hand. A gang fight would do more harm than good. He would have to act fast.

He stepped back, thrilled by the knowledge that Tony was won over and ready to side with him if necessary.

"I understand you're a pretty good boxer," Chip said coolly. "How about you and me settling this with gloves? Down at the Y or the PAL? That's a pretty good way to settle differences if they can't be ironed out intelligently, in a fair fight with gloves."

Rip laughed boisterously. "Now ain't that just like a college boy and social worker. We're s'posed to settle all this with a couple of pillows laced clear up to our elbows. What d'ya know about that, Skids?" His voice hardened. "Why at the Y, social worker? Why not down in the alley? Why not right now?"

"With gloves?"

"Sure! Sure, with gloves!" Rip cast an exaggerated wink in Skids's direction. "Go over to Moran's house, Skids, and get the gloves. You know, the real ones." He laughed sarcastically. "We gotta do this fair, ya know!"

UNDER THE ROCK

The crowd of boys suddenly broke for the alley, each anxious to get a good vantage point along the four-foot high wooden fence. Isaiah and Tony moved over and walked silently beside Chip as he moved down toward the alley. Up ahead, Rip and Bucky and several small admirers swaggered along.

Frank Caruso had heard the argument on the corner and had been surprised to see Chip. But he recognized trouble when he saw it, and, instead of interrupting, he left the cleaning of the store and hurried across the street to get Tony's father. Standing in the same doorway where Chip had paused was a formidable group of athletes who were watching the events unfold with special interest. Fireball and Whitty were all for barging in and breaking it up fast, but Biggie stopped them.

"Hold it!" Biggie commanded. "Chip wants it this way, or he'd have brought us along. Now you hold it, Fireball, Whitty. Chip can take care of himself. We'll move in if they gang up on him."

"That's right," Soapy agreed nervously. "Hold it."

"But we can't stand here and let him get beat up by a bunch of hoods," Fireball growled.

"They're not all hoods," Soapy protested. "Some of those kids are all right."

"We'll find out," Biggie said. "Come on. Don't make any noise."

With Biggie leading the way, they kept in the shadows of the buildings and found a spot in the alley across the street without being seen. From there they could see Chip and Isaiah, backed up against Caruso's garage, facing Rip and Bucky and the rest of the group lined up along the high wooden fence.

"Some odds," Speed whispered hoarsely. "What in the world is it all about?"

Part of Speed's question was answered right then. Skids returned and disdainfully tossed a pair of boxing gloves at Chip's feet. Then Skids began to lace the other pair on Rip's hands.

Once, Tony, Bucky, Isaiah, and others in that group had played games together in that alley, but no game and no argument had ever been quite as important as this one.

Brisk footsteps sounded down the narrow street. Frank Caruso and Tony's father appeared. "What's the trouble here?" Caruso demanded. "Mr. Chip, you OK?"

"I'm all right, Mr. Caruso. Rip Grasco and I are settling a little argument with boxing gloves."

"Not with those gloves," Caruso said, snatching one from Skids's hands. "Tony's dad told me about these gloves! Look at this! Look at this lead!"

Chip examined the glove. Sure enough, a short length of lead as thick as a broom handle had been sewn on the inside of the glove. "Real clever, Rip," he said. "Real fair too. A fair fight with gloves. Only your pair is loaded with lead weights!"

"You asked for it, sucker," Rip snarled. "What are you cryin' about, college boy?"

"I'm not crying. We'll settle this fifty-fifty. You take one and I'll take the other. Your choice."

Rip snorted gleefully. "I'll keep the one I got on," he said, banging his gloved right hand against the fence.

Frank Caruso helped Chip lace on his gloves. "You sure you wanna fight, Mr. Chip? I could call Pop King."

Chip shook his head. "No, Mr. Caruso, I'd rather settle it this way. I think we can settle a lot of things tonight."

"You said it, social worker," Skids said. "You're gonna settle right down on your back for a nice long sleep. Real soon now!"

UNDER THE ROCK

The boys who were lined up along the fence snickered at their leader's quip, but young Tony Carlara's face remained serious, his expression unchanged. The sturdy teenager hadn't said a word since Chip had joined the group on the corner. But Chip noticed that Tony was now surrounded by most of the kids in the group. A few others were standing farther down along the fence, beside Bucky.

Someone new had been added across the street. Pop King had appeared from nowhere, it seemed, startling everyone except Fireball and Soapy.

"Man, am I glad to see you!" Soapy whispered. "You gonna break it up?"

"No," King drawled. "I don't think so. We'll just see what happens."

The gloves were on now, and Chip advanced toward Rip and held out his gloved hands, palms down, in the traditional gesture of readiness. But Chip was facing a dirty fighter. Rip faked the touch and swung hard for Chip's jaw with the weighted right glove. But the glove merely whistled through the air as Chip drew back and instinctively stepped forward again with a hard left hook. The blow cracked flush against Rip's jaw, a square, jarring blow that thudded dully and half-dazed the snarling roughneck. Rip groaned and fell forward to his knees.

It had been a terrific shot with the loaded glove, and the fight ended right there as far as Rip was concerned. Chip turned away and held out his hands so the laces could be untied. Caruso went to work on one, and Isaiah eagerly began on the other.

"You never lead with a right, eh, Chip?" Isaiah chuckled.

Then it happened!

Skids leaped behind Chip and struck him over the head with a piece of wood. Chip tumbled forward as Rip gained his feet. Half-dazed, Chip fell to his knees and saw Rip, Skids, and Bucky attack Frank Caruso and Isaiah Redding.

"Old man, we'll teach you and these wimps to stick your nose in our business," Rip rasped, knocking Mr. Caruso to the ground. Skids grabbed Isaiah and slammed him hard against the wooden fence, and Bucky and Rip turned on Tony Carlara's father. The little man didn't have a chance against the two boys, and Rip shoved him to the ground.

"There!" Rip panted viciously. "I guess you know who's the boss around here now!"

Chip was struggling to get back on his feet, his head swimming and his thoughts reeling. He'd lost his big chance. Just when he nearly had the whole corner crowd turned around . . . .

In the alley on the other side of the street, Soapy was struggling with Pop King. "Wait, fellows," King said sharply. "Hold it!"

"But aren't you going to stop it?" Soapy demanded. "They haven't got a chance!"

"Just sit tight, sonny," King said. "There's more at stake than a couple of black eyes. Hilton can take care of himself, and unless I'm a rookie, this whole neighborhood is just about to wake up and take back what's theirs. Now watch!"

Chip had his senses back now and sprang to his feet. There was still a chance.

He rushed to help Mr. Caruso and Mr. Carlara just as Rip, Skids, and Bucky turned around. This time, Chip had help. Young Tony Caruso flashed past him like a panther and landed all over Skids Welks. And somehow,

UNDER THE ROCK

Mark Redding was right behind, rushing at Bucky Husta.

That left Rip Grasco. But before Chip could move, John Redding, still grimy from work, had knocked Grasco to the ground. With his arms folded across his chest, he straddled the bewildered ruffian. "I think it's time you crawled back under the rock you came out from under! This is our neighborhood and these are our kids. You and your kind don't belong here! You got it?"

Chip turned to help Mark and Tony, but it was all over. Skids was cowering on the ground with Tony standing over him, and Isaiah and Mark were holding a cringing Bucky against the garage door.

So as Pop King had said, a whole neighborhood had awakened and joined forces to take responsibility for what was important to them.

Pop King led the way, and as Chip's friends reached the scene, they heard Rip Grasco pleading for help from the bewildered kids who still lined the fence.

"C'mon, you guys," Rip pleaded in a hysterical voice. "C'mon, help us! We can take 'em!"

"You'd better help!" Skids threatened.

But Rip and Skids had been humiliated. They had lost the fight and their leadership, and the kids turned them down flat. Right then, Biggie gave the whole crowd of kids the greatest kick they would ever have— gave them something to talk about for months to come. Biggie winked at Pop King and said, "OK, I'll help you, buddy!"

Then he lifted Rip up in his arms and tossed him clear over the fence. Not to be outdone, Fireball grabbed Skids and threw him even higher and farther. Then he swooped down on Bucky. "How about this one?" he cried.

Isaiah Redding shook his head. "Never mind him," he said firmly. "I can handle him from now on." He walked between Tony and Mark and jerked Bucky to his feet. "Right?" he demanded.

"Right, Isaiah," Bucky said. "Right!"

The kids had doubled over with laughter at the sight of Rip and Skids sailing over the fence, but there was also a great deal of awe in their faces. Then, as Biggie, Fireball, Whitty, Soapy, Speed, and Red crowded around Chip, the kids recognized the invaders.

"I know you!" one boy cried, tugging at Biggie's arm. "You're Biggie Cohen! No wonder you could throw Rip over the fence!"

"Yeah, and the other guy is Fireball Finley!" another cried. "The fullback!"

Frank Caruso made the move that broke up the excitement. "Come on," he cried, grabbing Chip by the arm. "We all go to my friend Tony's house. Come on, Mr. Redding, you come too! Come on, you footballs, we have some wine!"

Soapy started to explain that they didn't drink and then stopped in the middle of his sentence. "Hey," he cried, "come on! It's after midnight! We're in trouble. We gotta run for it!"

"I've got to go, too," Chip told Mr. Caruso and Mr. Carlara.

"But we're going to organize a club for the kids," Mr. Carlara protested. "Mr. Redding and Frank and me and Pop King and—"

"Yeah," Caruso interrupted, "and we're going to call it the Mr. Chip Club!"

Chip promised to be back the next day, and he and his teammates sprinted up Tenth Street.

If someone sees us now— Soapy thought.

UNDER THE ROCK

At Tenth and Main, a string of cars from both directions were stopped for the red light. Chip's crowd breathed a sigh and made a dash to cross the street.

Halfway across, Soapy stopped dead in his tracks, completely demoralized. "Oh, no!" he moaned. "Look! The coach's car! And the coach is in it!"

"That's not who I see looking at me," Biggie drawled as he pulled Soapy from the middle of the street.

CHAPTER 20

The Neighborhood Expedition

HENRY ROCKWELL couldn't believe his eyes. "Biggie? It can't be," he said incredulously. "Chip, Soapy, Biggie, Speed, Red, and—why, almost every sophomore on the squad! It's not possible!"

"Where in the world could they have been?" Jim Sullivan asked. When neither of his companions replied, he muttered half aloud, "Now what?"

Each of the three coaches was thinking of the men who had accompanied them to Cleveland and who had been in the car behind them when they stopped for the red light at Main and Tenth. The head coach was the one to break the silence.

"Nothing else to do," Ralston muttered. "Got to do it! Well, let's get it over with." He braked the car to a stop and led the way into the Campus Restaurant and to a booth in the corner. Bill Bell and Jim Locke were right on his heels, smelling a story and anxious to be in on the ground floor. "Did you see—" Locke began.

"Yes, I saw," Ralston said calmly, "but I don't know anymore about it than you do."

"Curfew in effect?" Bell asked.

Ralston nodded. "Yes," he said slowly. "Eleven o'clock."

"Sure caught them red-handed," Locke said slyly. "Or rather flatfooted. Any comment?"

Ralston chewed at his lower lip and thought it over. "No," he said shortly, "I guess not."

"But they're ineligible as of now," Locke persisted.

"Yes," Ralston said, "until I get a reasonable explanation."

"What's reasonable?" Locke demanded.

Ralston rose abruptly. "Jim, I can't answer that right now," he said coolly. "I guess I won't wait for coffee. Good night."

"But what about a statement?" Locke persisted. "What—"

But Ralston was gone, leaving the group to speculate and each to form his own opinion. Rockwell and Sullivan were tight-lipped and would make no comment. Soon the group split up, confused and disturbed to varying degrees.

Locke broke the story with a headline in the *News* the next morning, filling his column with suppositions and nasty speculations about the "red-handed apprehension." He went on to state, in his opinion, "the suspension of the sophomore sleepwalkers might be a blessing in disguise. Ralston will now be forced to rely on his veterans and that will give State an outside chance for an upset."

Soapy got an early copy of the paper and brought it back as evidence of his dire forebodings. At nine o'clock Chip and his friends met to decide the proper course of action. While they were talking, Soapy again scurried out to get sandwiches and coffee.

"Good thing we're on vacation," he reported when he returned. "We'd probably be run off the campus. It's all over town! Only thing people are talking about! What're we gonna do?"

"*We* are not going to do anything," Chip said pointedly. "It was my personal project, and *I'm* going to report to Coach Ralston and assume full responsibility. It was my fault and mine alone."

"That's not true," Cohen said gently. "None of us had to go, Chip. We went because we *wanted* to go. There's a big difference."

Try as he might, Chip could not shake his friends on that point, and they were right behind him when he reported to Coach Ralston's secretary at ten o'clock. The head coach and his two assistants were waiting when the players filed into the office.

Chip got right to the point. "I guess you know why we're here, Coach," he said. "I'd like to first explain, sir, that the rest of the guys were only trying to help me out of a difficulty."

"That's not quite correct, Coach," Biggie corrected. "We all knew exactly what we were doing, and we're just as responsible as Chip."

"Just what is it all about?" Ralston asked.

"It's a personal matter, sir," Chip said. "The rest of the guys thought that I might get into trouble."

"What sort of a personal matter?"

"It's hard to explain, Coach. It was something I didn't have to do and still had to do. It's rather mixed up."

"But you don't seem to understand, Chip. I *have* to have some sort of an explanation. Otherwise, you leave me no alternative. I'll be forced to suspend the whole group."

"But I'm the only one concerned, sir."

"And you won't disclose the reason for breaking the curfew?"

"I'd rather not, sir."

Ralston shook his head. "I don't understand it." He turned to the others. "How about you men? Any explanation to make?"

There was no answer. Ralston sighed and rose slowly to his feet. "Then you force me to drop all of you from the squad," he said, turning wearily away. "That's all."

"Now what do we do?" Soapy asked when they reached the street.

"I know what I'm going to do," Chip said disconsolately. "I'm going home."

"Valley Falls?" Soapy said incredulously. "And face your mom and all your friends? Not me!"

"That's up to you," Chip said. "But that's where I'm going."

"When do we leave?" Soapy said in a subdued voice.

Chip turned to Fireball and Whitty. "Mom was expecting us Thursday night after the game," he said, smiling regretfully. "I guess it's all right if we show up a little early. That is, if you still want to go."

"We wouldn't go anywhere else," Whitty and Fireball chorused. "We can call our parents from your house. Let's go!"

"All right!" Speed barked. "Biggie and I'll get the limos."

Within an hour, seven State athletes and best friends had packed their books and dirty laundry into two cars and with mixed feelings headed for the interstate and Valley Falls. Two hours later they pulled into the driveway of 131 Beech Street, feeling down about football and their teammates, but right about so much more.

Mary Hilton had taken a vacation day to get everything ready for Chip and his college friends. It was mid-afternoon when she heard footsteps on the front porch. Through the glass panels on each side of the wooden door, she could see Chip wrestling with his door key, laundry bag, and bookbag slung over his shoulder.

Her heart leaped as she opened the door. Without a moment's hesitation, Chip dropped his bags and caught his mom up in his arms, giving her their familiar carousel-like twirl and hug. Chip kissed her as he put her lightly down, and then she turned and welcomed the boys.

Soapy gave her a quick hug before his nose led him to the kitchen, with Hoops meowing and trailing behind him. Soon they were all seated in the kitchen enjoying early Thanksgiving desserts of pumpkin pie, apple pie, and Soapy's favorite, double chocolate cake.

"What happened, Chip?" Mary Hilton asked. "All I could get on the radio, TV, and in the papers was something about all of you being suspended for breaking training rules."

Chip told his mom the story from beginning to end while his buddies listened. "So that's it, Mom," he concluded. "There wasn't much of a choice."

"You did just right," his mother said. "I'm proud of you, proud of all of you, and I know your parents will be also when you tell them. But why couldn't you tell the coach what you just told me? Wouldn't he understand?"

Chip nodded. "He'd understand, all right, Mom. But a guy can't ask for sympathy or take credit for helping a friend. I just couldn't do it. It would sound like trying to be a hero or something like that. I don't care for myself, but it isn't right for the rest of the guys to suffer just because they wanted to help *me*."

"You wanted to help Isaiah, didn't you?" Biggie said softly. "Well, we're no different, Chip. We wanted to help you, and we wanted to act on our friendship, just like you wanted to act on your friendship for Isaiah."

Soapy changed the subject. "Bet the rest of the team would like to see us now," he chortled, snaring another big piece of cake as Hoops rubbed against his legs. "Training is OK, but you can't beat the simple pleasures of life."

Back in University at the pizzeria, Frank Caruso was struggling with Bill Bell's story in the *Herald* while Isaiah, Mark, Tony, Bucky, and the rest of the kids listened in mournful silence.

STATE STARS DISCIPLINED
FOR CHAMPIONSHIP GAME
State Loses Seven Sophomore Stars
For Training Irregularities
by Bill Bell

Chip "Mister Toe" Hilton, Biggie Cohen, Soapy Smith, Philip Whittemore, Red Schwartz, Speed Morris, and Fireball Finley are suspended for training violations.

Coach Curly Ralston announced today that seven of State's varsity players had been suspended for an infraction of training rules. The seven players failed to observe the eleven o'clock curfew rule that has been in effect all season.

It is the second offense for Chip Hilton, who had been benched for the game with the Dukes as a penalty.

Coach Ralston had journeyed to Cleveland last evening to attend a coaches meeting and was returning with assistant coaches Henry Rockwell and Jim Sullivan late last night. At the corner of Main and Tenth streets, Ralston stopped for a red light. At that precise moment, the seven players crossed the street. It was then 12:30 A.M.

The players reported to Ralston's office this morning, and when no satisfactory explanation was given, Curly Ralston suspended the players.

Coach Ralston said he regretted the necessity for the action but that discipline and sportsmanship are as important in football as in everyday life and that a player who violates training rules without an exceptional reason has betrayed a trust and must be disciplined for the good of the game and his teammates.

The State varsity left for Archton this morning and will work out late this afternoon on the A & M freshman practice field.

As soon as Frank Caruso finished reading the paper, Mark leaped to his feet. "You gotta do something, Isaiah," he pleaded earnestly. "Chip and the whole bunch got in trouble on account of *you!*"

"Me?"

"Yes, you! I called Chip and told him that Rip and Skids were gonna beat you up last night. That's why he showed up."

Isaiah was shocked. "You mean you snitched!"

"Call it that if you want. Anyway, it ain't snitchin'. Chip said so. I told Chip and I told Pop when he came home from work. That's why Chip and Pop showed up."

"Now I get it," Isaiah said. "Wasn't Pop great? I've been trying all day to figure out how come Chip and all the football guys showed up. Sure we gotta do something! We gotta see the coach. We gotta see Ralston!"

"But the team's gone," Tony said. "They left this morning for A & M. It says that right in the paper."

"Then we gotta get to A & M!"

"What you going to use for money?" Tony asked. "You gonna beam yourself there?"

Frank Caruso had been listening intently. Now he broke into the conversation. "We take the truck," he said excitedly.

"I don't think we can all fit in the truck, Mr. Caruso," Tony announced.

"You're right," Mr. Caruso nodded. "Tony, your brother Angelo has a van. He can drive. Run, Tony! Tell your father his friend Frank Caruso wants to see him."

It was after midnight before the last passenger was home from work and the neighborhood expedition was completely organized. But at last the group was off. Angelo Carlara at the wheel of his van, Mr. Caruso in the front passenger seat as navigator, Mr. and Mrs. Carlara with John Redding, still dressed in his work clothes, in the middle row bench seat, and Tony, Isaiah, Mark, and Bucky somehow squeezed into the rear section with the snacks and luggage.

Angelo Carlara triumphantly drove into Archton early the next morning and sped down the main street just as if he knew where he was going. But he didn't. It was Thanksgiving morning and nearly everything was closed. The University neighbors had no idea where the State team was staying, so it took them almost two hours of driving from hotel to hotel to finally locate Curly Ralston and the team at the Hotel Western.

Angelo parked right in front of the hotel and five minutes later had an assistant coach on the house phone. It took several repetitions of the story to convince the skeptical coach that Coach Ralston needed to hear this story.

When Ralston finally got on the phone, he was bewildered by the garbled explanation but recognized the urgency in Carlara's voice and hurried down to the lobby. There he was immediately surrounded by the neighborhood contingent, each member loudly trying to tell him the story.

While all this was going on in Archton, Chip and his friends were over on the high school field working out with the Valley Falls team. After a while, Chip borrowed a ball and they began to practice Tims Lansing's play.

It was just 9:45 when Taps Browning, Chip's next-door neighbor, came dashing out onto the football field. Taps's long legs were flying. "Hey, Chip!" he yelled excitedly. "You hear the news? It's on radio and TV and all over! You've been reinstated! The whole bunch of you!"

Chip was sure Taps had gotten it wrong. "What do you mean? How do you know?"

Soapy frowned. "Taps, even *I* don't think that's funny."

"No, really!" Taps repeated, "I heard it on TV not five minutes ago. Saw it myself! Seems some group showed up in Archton and told the coach and the papers and anyone else who'd listen what happened."

When Chip saw his mom's car, with the headlights flashing, pulling into the high school parking lot, he began to comprehend what Taps was saying and ran toward the car.

"Chip," Mary Hilton called, "Coach Rockwell just phoned and wants to talk to you. Wants to talk to all of you. He's calling again in about ten minutes. C'mon! Hurry!"

"Yahoo!" Soapy squealed, tossing the football up in the air and yelling to the State players on the field. "C'mon, you guys! C'mon, Speed, let's get this junk pile movin'!"

On the way, Taps told how he had been watching a sports program from Archton. The sportscaster was interviewing the A & M coach when the station broke it off and announced that Coach Ralston had reinstated his sophomores—except that he didn't know where they were.

"Then the sportscaster got all these kids on the screen and said they were friends of Chip Hilton. One of the boys told about you getting him out of trouble, and then the sportscaster introduced the boy's father and mother and brother and three other boys, and that's when I took off!"

Fireball elbowed Browning in the ribs and Taps winced. "You better not be kidding," he said.

"On my honor."

Red laughed. "Fireball, it's got to be true; even Soapy couldn't make up a story like this!"

Speed's red Mustang pulled into the driveway right behind Mary Hilton's car just as Biggie pulled up to the curb in front of the house. Every player was out of the cars, into the house, and staring at the phone before Mary Hilton had a chance to take her seat belt off!

R-I-N-G!

The players held their breath as Chip answered the phone. Coach Henry Rockwell's relieved voice came loud and sharp and excited through the receiver. "Chip! Everything's all right! Haven't got time to explain it right now, but you've all been reinstated. Are the other players with you?"

"Yes, Coach, they're all right beside me."

"Good! Since you're all reinstated, Coach Ralston expects each of you to be in Aggie Stadium for the game."

"Great! How can we get there in time for the game?"

"We've checked the airline schedules. There's a flight from Valley Falls to here with one stop, and there's enough seats for all of you. Now, you know, each of you will have to pay your own way. After all, the team bus came with everyone else yesterday as planned."

"I understand, Coach."

"Coach Ralston will have the bus drive to the Archton airport to meet the flight, but you seven will have to pay the bus company for those charges too. Coach Ralston will send a manager on the bus with all your uniforms and equipment. You'll have to hurry. Come right to the Aggie Stadium."

"Coach, if we get there in time, do you think we might get in the game?"

"Well, Chip, that's up to Coach Ralston. I'll be looking for you guys. Be careful now!"

"Thanks, Coach, you can count on us!" Then Chip hung up the phone and faced the expectant stares of his teammates and his mom.

"Coach says we're back on the team, and they expect us to join the rest of the team at A & M for the game."

A loud celebration of shouts, whoops, and high-fives greeted his happy news, followed by a barrage of questions.

"Can we play?"

"All of us?"

"When do we leave?"

"Coach Ralston wants us to pay?"

"How can we get there in time?"

"Who's got extra money?"

"What are we waiting for?"

"Can we take the Thanksgiving turkey with us?"

Chip filled everyone in on the high points of his conversation with the Rock, and then Mary Hilton set things in motion.

"I can call the airline to reserve your seats. Everyone except Whitty and Fireball go home and tell your parents where you're going and get the money for your flight and the bus. If Biggie's brother Abe can drive one car, I'll drive another to the airport. Be back here as quickly as you can."

Her words were barely out of her mouth when bodies began flying toward the front door and up the stairs.

Chip yelled back as he was racing up the steps, "Bring extra money for Fireball and Whitty!"

"There go my tips for the rest of the year!" Soapy pretended to moan as he jumped into Speed's Mustang.

Just when it seemed the Hilton house couldn't get anymore hectic, the phone rang again.

"Maybe we shouldn't answer it in case Coach Ralston's changed his mind," Fireball murmured as Whitty answered the phone.

"Hey, Chip, it's for you. It's some girl."

CHAPTER 21

Friends

"HI, LEAH. Sure I remember you," Chip responded.

"I've been trying to find you since yesterday," Leah began. "I called Grayson's, and they thought you went to the game. But I knew that was wrong. Then I tracked down Mitzi, and she said you lived on campus in Jefferson Hall. Some grouchy guy there said you probably went home to Valley Falls. So I called information to get this number."

"What's so important for you to spend all that time looking for me?" Chip questioned.

"Well, Rosie Carlara, Tony's sister—we play soccer together—stayed with me last night since her parents left late last night for the football game."

"Well, Leah," Chip chuckled, "that sure clears up some things I heard about this morning."

"Anyway," she continued, "Rosie told me something important, and that's why I called."

Leah went on to tell Chip about Rip Grasco's and

Skids Welks's scheme to rob Grayson's and pin it on Isaiah, Tony, and Bucky. After the big problem in the alley on Tuesday night, Rosie had overheard Mr. Carlara, Tony, and Bucky talking about the night the boys were told they had to prove their loyalty by taking Mr. Caruso's truck and parking it near Grayson's on Tenth Street. At the time, the boys thought taking the truck was just a prank that would get them in good graces with the new leaders in the neighborhood.

But later, Bucky overheard Rip and Skids talking. They had told the boys to take the truck and park it near Grayson's and then leave. Later that night, Rip and Skids had planned to break into Grayson's and load up the truck. They would make some easy money selling the stolen items and at the same time pay back that meddling Chip Hilton for making friends on their turf and interfering in their neighborhood.

Since Isaiah worked at Grayson's and the boys were friends, it would look like Isaiah, Tony, and Bucky were guilty. No one would ever link Rip and Skids to the stolen truck or theft.

"So, that's why I called, Chip. I hope you don't mind being bothered on your holiday," Leah paused.

"Not at all, I'm glad you did call and—"

Leah interrupted. "There's more. Rosie wants me to tell you how thankful she is that you're her brother's friend. If you hadn't stopped those three idiots that night, who knows what would have happened to them."

Biggie stuck his head in the front door just as Chip hung up the phone. "Anyone in here wanna play football today?"

"I'm sorry, Mr. Smith, but we don't have a seat for you—"

"Oh, no! But I—er—we've got reservations! You *have* to have a seat for me!" Soapy winced, practically in tears.

"What I was *trying* to say was, we don't have a seat for you with the rest of your group. But there is one seat in an upgraded class, if you want it," the flight attendant responded coldly.

Soapy's entire demeanor changed. "Upgrade? Absolutely! Soapy Smith is finally going first class!"

On the plane, Soapy kept sticking his head out from behind the cabin's dividing curtain to look back at his friends. He stuck his thumbs in his ears and gleefully wiggled his fingers to each of them. Each time he caught Biggie's eyes and wiggled those fingers, the big tackle would smile, point first at Soapy, then to the overhead bin directly above his seat. Somehow, Soapy always found a way to brighten difficult moments.

Chip watched the exchanges between his traveling teammates and thought about friendship. He remembered how Coach Ralston had often said one game does not make a season. More importantly, Chip also knew that one act of friendship can change a life. His life had been blessed many times by each one of these friends and many others.

Gloom was a foot thick in the State sections of the A & M oval. It was the end of the third quarter. The reason for the depression of the State fans loomed in large, eye-catching numerals right at the open end of the stadium for every fan in the place to see: A & M 9, State 6.

The State veterans had put up a terrific fight in the bitter battle, but it had been apparent early in the first half that the power to blast the tough A & M scoring zone was missing. But the State fans never gave up hope. They had been encouraged by the reports that Chip

FRIENDS

Hilton and the talented sophomores had been reinstated and would play, and they kept watching the State entrance to the field all afternoon.

A & M had scored on a touchdown and a safety while State had capitalized on the recovery of an Aggies fumble on the ten-yard line in the third quarter for their only score. Ace Gibbons had punched his way across for the touchdown in four tries but had failed on the try for the extra point. That had been the last time State had gotten close to pay dirt.

Gee-Gee Gray was doing his best to encourage the State fans. Back in University, in Frank Caruso's pizzeria, Pop King and half the neighborhood had crowded around the TV ever since the startling and almost unbelievable news had spread along Tenth Street. The Carlara and Redding families and Bucky Husta had been on TV that morning from Archton.

It was the same in Grayson's and in the PAL Center on Main Street. Lieutenant Byrnes divided his time between watching the game and completing his paperwork. And in Valley Falls, at the Sugar Bowl and in the headquarters of the Hilton Athletic Club, it was the same. Mary Hilton, home from the airport, had the game going in the family room and the radio blasting away in the kitchen. And Mr. and Mrs. Browning, Taps, Suzy, and a whole group of the Valley Falls kids who knew Chip were parked in front of the TV, watching and waiting to see if the guys would get to the game before it ended.

Somehow, the fans had sensed the players' arrival even before they dashed out onto the field. Two members of the A & M field security got the biggest cheer they would ever hear when they led seven recently dressed sophomores to the State sideline.

State had the ball on its own thirty-yard line, second down and nine, with five minutes left to play, when Mike Brennan heard the thunderous roar and called a time-out.

In one glance, Chip took in the score, the position of the ball on the field, and the time left to play. Then Coach Curly Ralston shook his hand and nearly tore his arm out of the socket when he swung Chip right out on the field. The head coach did the same with each of the other six players, and they tore out to report. The veterans gave them a welcome cheer and pounded them on the backs. Those they replaced trotted off the field giving high-fives and leaving no doubt in anyone's mind how they felt about these teammates.

Everyone in the stadium was standing—the State fans cheering like only State fans can cheer, and the Aggies fans joined in the uproar because they were carried away by the drama of the moment.

The A & M players stood with their hands on their hips, their expressions curious and appraising. "So the *stars* have arrived to win the game," one remarked sarcastically.

"You'll be seeing stars," Soapy retorted, "on the first play!"

Chip passed to Whittemore before the Aggies knew he had the ball, and Whitty went way up in the air to pull the toss down on the State forty-five. Then Fireball tore through the middle for twelve vital yards to put the ball on the A & M forty-three-yard line, and the Aggies captain called time. State fans grew louder.

When time was in, Chip sent Speed tearing through left tackle for four yards. Then he passed again to Whittemore on a buttonhook that was good for seven and the first down. The Aggies captain again called time.

FRIENDS

During the time-out, Chip studied the clock, the position of the ball, and the path to the goal line thirty-two yards away. There was time for only a few more plays, he was thinking. What to do? What would Tims Lansing do in this situation?

The field judge waved, and Chip called the play in the huddle.

Finley took off on the quick-opening play like a jet but didn't gain an inch. The official whistled an end to the play, but the big Aggies line continued and carried him back for five yards before he toppled to the ground and was buried under an avalanche of bodies. The Aggies fans really liked that! Fireball took a long time getting up, shaking his head and holding his shoulder. The referee brought the ball back to the A & M thirty-two-yard line, squarely in the middle of the field, and Mike Brennan called time.

It was second down now, and Chip once again glanced at the clock. "We've got to stay in the center of the field," he muttered.

In the huddle he called for a pass into the end zone. "Thirty-three X on two, guys," he said. Then he looked at Whittemore. "I'm going to throw it high, Whitty. We can't risk an interception."

Time was in then, and the roar from the stands came booming around Chip.

He faded back, faked to Speed in the flat, and barely got the ball away. But it was too high! The ball sailed above Whittemore's hands and out of bounds behind the end zone.

Chip again glanced at the clock. "Thirty-one! Crossbuck, guys. All yours, Fireball. On three, let's go!"

Chip faked to Gibbons, pivoted quickly, and gave Fireball the ball. But the Aggies linebacker broke through and tackled Fireball just as he got the handoff. Fireball fought his way back to the line, and Chip cast a frantic glance at the clock and yelled, "Time!" Fourth down. No more time-outs. Time for all or nothing. One last play! It was a fourth-down showdown!

Chip looked at the scoreboard and studied the clock and the big numerals: A & M 9, State 6. Then he walked over behind the ball and sighted the line to the goal. Once more his thoughts turned to Tims Lansing. What would Tims do *now* if he were calling the plays? Would Tims try for the tie and maybe go into overtime, or would he go for the win?

Tims would go all the way, Chip breathed to himself. *All the way! Wouldn't it be great if his play could win the game?* He sighted the line from the ball to the goal once more and then hustled back to the huddle. On the way he passed the referee and without looking at the man he whispered sharply, "Special play coming up! Please watch!" Then he knelt in the center of the huddle. "Time for one last play, guys. It's now or never."

Mike Brennan slapped him on the back. "You can do it, Chipper. We'll hold 'em!"

"You got that right!" Finley rasped. "You can kick this one blindfolded!"

Chip shook his head. "We're not kicking!" he whispered cautiously. "We're playing to win!"

The circle tightened as the import of the words struck home. "Now listen," Chip said sharply, "we're going to use Tims Lansing's play, the fake kick! Everyone know it?"

"*We* oughta know it," Soapy said. "We practiced it all morning."

"Speed can do it," Chip continued, "but he's got to have good blocking. Fireball's got to get the end, Biggie takes the tackle, and Whitty's got to handle their left deep defender."

He grabbed Mike Brennan by the arm. "That leaves the key block for you, Mike. You've got to get downfield and block the right cornerback for Speed." He turned to Speed. "Be sure to have *both* knees *off* the ground when you catch the ball! Well, that's it! Go get 'em, guys!"

Chip and Mike clasped hands and the team joined in the grip. "This one is for Tims," Chip gritted. "On the count of three, team! Let's go!"

Most football crowds start for the exits when there are only seconds to play. But these fans were different. The annual State-A & M game was the game of any week and any year for them. And this game today was one of the greatest of all time. They stood tense and immobile as State came out of the huddle and lined up for the field goal. The Aggies fans began to chant, "Block that kick!"

When Chip lined up the kick and dropped back, the chant grew to a tremendous roar. The rhythmic thunder of "Block that kick! Block that kick! Block that kick!" caught up the whole crowd. For a moment, even the State fans were tempted to join in the chorus, although that would have meant going against their own team.

The thundering roar seemed a greater obstacle to Chip than the players on the field. It seemed to build up a wall between the ball and the precious goal line thirty-two yards away. Thirty-two long, desperately long, yards, plus ten more to clear the crossbar above the end-zone line. Chip concentrated on the spot Speed had chosen. It was directly at the center of the crossbar. Chip tried with every bit of his being to feel, to *know*, that he was going to kick the ball squarely between the uprights.

The ball came spinning back to Speed, true and fast, and the mighty roar from the stands seemed to lift the

A & M forwards over and through the State line as if it were paper. The groan of anguish from the State fans almost equaled the home cheers as the big linemen charged toward Chip.

Chip stepped forward, concentrating on the ball for all it was worth, and kicked right through Speed's arms. Then he lifted his head and eyes as though watching the ball in flight. Just before the Aggies forwards hurled him to the ground, he heard a tremendous shout of dismay from the A & M fans and turned his head just in time to glimpse Speed tearing around left end and heading for pay dirt only yards away.

The big linemen buried him under their massive bodies then, but Chip heard the exultant roar of the State fans. He never saw Speed cross the goal line, untouched, and hand the ball to the official just as the game clock ran out. State 12, A & M 9! But he knew Tims Lansing's play, which he and his friends had practiced so carefully that morning in Valley Falls, had worked. He knew all of them had performed their parts perfectly.

Up in the broadcast booth, Gee-Gee Gray gave a piercing shout into his headset just as Speed crossed the goal line. He let the roar of the State fans tell the story to his listeners. And just a few feet away, Jim Locke grimaced and shouted, "Lucky! Suppose it hadn't worked?"

Bill Bell grinned and shouted back, "But it did!"

Chip knew there were sixty thousand spectators in the stadium, but he didn't know that thirty million other game-of-the-week viewers saw his teammates hoist Speed and himself to their shoulders and carry them around and around the field.

High up in the concrete bowl, Mr. Carlara was holding a copy of the *Herald* in his hand and showing anyone who would look the picture of Chip and his buddies.

"That's my boy!" he shouted. "Tony and Angelo, here, they're my boys. But this one"—he poked his finger at Chip's picture—"this one, he's my boy too!"

Chip would have enjoyed hearing Mr. Carlara say that and also would have liked to see the proud expressions on the faces of Isaiah, Mark, Tony, John Redding, and Bucky Husta. But right then, he was riding on a wave of shoulders. And back in the line of celebrants, he could see Speed and Soapy and Captain Mike Brennan and Fireball and Whitty and Larry Higgins and Red Schwartz and Biggie Cohen and Ace Gibbons bouncing along as though riding a string of camels.

Curly Ralston and Rock and Jim Sullivan were standing up on the bench waving and yelling, and a video crew was trying to get their attention. Then the crews saw Chip and fought their way through the crowds. The announcer held the mike up to him and shouted, "Here, Hilton, say something! Say anything! You couldn't say anything wrong right now if you tried. Say hello to your mom or your friends! Go on!"

Chip took the mike with the long trailing cord and said, "Hello, Mom, looks like we made it!" Then he grinned self-consciously and said to himself, "As if she doesn't know!" Then he remembered the fake-kick play and said, "Hello, Tims Lansing! Your play won the game! Hello, Mr. Grayson! Hello, Mr. Caruso! Hello, Mitzi! Hello, Pop King!"

Then Soapy came bouncing along, and the announcer gave him the mike. But all Soapy would say was, "Move over, Florida! Move over, Georgia! Move over, Nebraska! Move over, Oklahoma! You got company! You got State University company!"

FOURTH DOWN SHOWDOWN

• • •

Chip Hilton and Jimmy Chung, a wizard of a ball-handler, wage a fierce contest for a starting assignment on State's basketball team. But when ill fortune forces Jimmy to leave State, Chip and the guys devise a plan that merges Eastern filial piety and Western teamwork. The plan succeeds just in time for State to meet another crisis in the Holiday International Tournament. The most unusual Chip Hilton story to date, *Tournament Crisis* is a must read!

Afterword

A LOT of kids hope to be a Yankee or a Dodger. I wanted to be a Valley Falls Big Red or State U. Statesman and be on Chip's team. And in my mind, I was. Through the annual rereadings of all the books, I was part of Chip's world. And I considered Clair Bee the kindly uncle supplementing my already elite education about sportsmanship and life.

To those of us who were raised loving both sports and storytelling, reading *The Scarlet Pimpernel* and *Huckleberry Finn* and the then-latest Chip book, Clair Bee was one of our coaches. We were vicariously a part of his world. Maybe it was even more than vicarious. In those days, our imaginations were more powerful, undiluted by adult cynicism. I read the books annually after inheriting a few from my older brother Dave and adding to the collection myself.

I wrote my name inside the front cover. In ink.

I fell asleep with *Clutch Hitter* on the bed. Darn it,

there were only ninety-six pages left, and I thought I could make it through it. And some of those crinkled pages in the family collections were the result of rolling over onto the book in the middle of the night.

I scribbled the date of each reading in pencil on the back endpapers until my list looked like a list of birthdays of all my classmates. I scribbled a moustache onto Chip as he followed through on his swing on the *Home Run Feud* cover.

I can't ever remember where I put my wallet, but I never forgot the name of Chip's Japanese pal from *No-Hitter*. (Right, Tamio?)

But, most of all, I learned.

I didn't completely understand how wonderful it was that Coach Bee didn't condescend, that he gave all of us credit for intelligence in challenging us. The world he created was a fantasy, yes. But as heroic as Chip could be, as fulfilling and tidy as the resolutions were, did we ever feel for a second that Clair Bee was playing a trick on us? I didn't. There were conflicts, racism, bumps in the road, bad guys, illnesses, malevolent sportswriters, and dirty opponents, and never, not for one second, did I feel as if I was misled and fooled. And here's the amazing thing: After reaching middle age, after seeing the best and worst of sports for all these years, I still feel that Clair Bee and Chip were being straight with me.

I've been around sports my entire life, as the son of a coach, as an athlete of modest ability and multiple knee operations, as a sportswriter who finally was forgiven—about eleven minutes ago—by his family for taking up that dishonorable profession. (Yes, yes, I know Chip was thinking of becoming a sportswriter, but I also believe he would have reconsidered.)

My dad, Jerry Frei, climbed the coaching ladder from

high school to college and ultimately to the National Football League as a longtime offensive line coach with several teams. Ultimately, he was a scout and then the director of college scouting for the Denver Broncos.

I can say without blushing that two of the more heartwarming experiences in my life were attending two reunions and tributes with him. The first was the fiftieth reunion of the 1949 Oregon state high school champions, Portland's Grant Generals, for whom my father was assistant coach in his first job. The second was a tribute put on for him by many of his former University of Oregon players and assistant coaches—a cast that includes Hall of Fame quarterback Dan Fouts, broadcaster Ahmad Rashad, and Redskins coach Norv Turner. It also includes Oregon former assistant coaches George Seifert, John Robinson, and Bruce Snyder.

Why do I bring that up?

Because I came to realize that even in a career that would lead to my father wearing a Super Bowl championship ring—as an administrator for the Broncos—his most important contribution was just being himself. Honorable and straightforward. Which is what Clair Bee preached all along. I've heard it said that Jerry Frei wasn't ruthless enough to be a "great" head coach, which I think is unfair; but I also take it as a compliment. Let's put it this way, in Hilton terms. My dad could have coached at State University, but he couldn't have survived long at the underhanded rival school, Southwestern. Know what? I've made comparisons and composed analogies along those "Chip" lines all my life, even if most of the time just to myself.

So I've had two Henry Rockwells in my life, one in my own house and one in my bookcase and imagination. It's almost as if they were in parallel universes, one real, one imagined, and both illuminating. Although Chip's prowess was mythical, I've been around great athletes all my life and had my own "Hilton A. C." gang as I was growing up. Remember when that wasn't a pejorative term? But I think that enhanced the experience of these books, and I daresay a lot of "kids" my age could identify with that.

As I detoured into journalism, writing mainly for the *Denver Post* and the *Sporting News,* I was exposed to a myriad of athletes, coaches, and events that could sour me on sports. I can be as cynical as anyone in the business, but I have Chip and Clair Bee and my father and his players and his coaches to thank—all of them—for helping show me how it could be. How it should be. And while we all know that Chip was in the fiction section, I keep finding the examples, more examples than we are willing to acknowledge in a cynical age, of how there still are strains of Chip and Rock and the gang all the way through sports.

So now, as I keep looking at the old books, as I talk with other Chip fans who have had similar feelings (pity the non-Chip fan who is the third at a dinner table with two Chip fans going through the plots), as I hope a new generation will discover Chip and his values, I thank Clair Bee maybe twenty-three times a week.

TERRY FREI
Sportswriter,
The Denver Post

Your Score Card

I have   I expect
read: to read:

____   ____   1. ***Touchdown Pass:*** The first story in the
                    series, introducing you to William "Chip"
                    Hilton and all his friends at Valley Falls High
                    during an exciting football season.

____   ____   2. ***Championship Ball:*** With a broken
                    ankle and an unquenchable spirit, Chip
                    wins the state basketball championship and
                    an even greater victory over himself.

____   ____   3. ***Strike Three!*** In the hour of his team's
                    greatest need, Chip Hilton takes to the
                    mound and puts the Big Reds in line for all-
                    state honors.

____   ____   4. ***Clutch Hitter!*** Chip's summer job at
                    Mansfield Steel Company gives him a chance
                    to play baseball on the famous Steelers team
                    where he uses his head as well as his war club.

____   ____   5. ***A Pass and a Prayer:*** Chip's last football
                    season is a real challenge as conditions for
                    the Big Reds deteriorate. Somehow he must
                    keep the team together for the coach.

____   ____   6. ***Hoop Crazy:*** When three-point fever
                    spreads to the Valley Falls basketball var-
                    sity, Chip Hilton has to do something, and
                    fast!

FOURTH DOWN SHOWDOWN

I have   I expect
read: to read:

____   ____   7. **Pitchers' Duel:** Valley Falls participates
                      in the state baseball tournament, and Chip
                      Hilton pitches in a nineteen-inning struggle
                      fans will long remember. The Big Reds year-
                      end banquet isn't to be missed!

____   ____   8. **Dugout Jinx:** Chip is graduated and has
                      one more high school game before beginning
                      a summer internship with a minor-league
                      team during its battle for the league pennant.

____   ____   9. **Freshman Quarterback:** Early autumn
                      finds Chip Hilton and four of his Valley Falls
                      friends at Camp Sundown, the temporary site
                      of State University's freshman and varsity
                      football teams. Join them in Jefferson Hall to
                      share successes, disappointments, and pranks.

____   ____   10. **Backboard Fever:** It's nonstop basket-
                      ball excitement! Chip and Mary Hilton face a
                      personal crisis. The Bollingers discover what
                      it means to be a family, but not until tragedy
                      strikes their two sons.

____   ____   11. **Fence Busters:** Can the famous freshman
                      baseball team live up to the sportswriter's
                      nickname or will it fold? Will big egos and an
                      injury to Chip Hilton divide the team? Can a
                      beanball straighten out an errant player?

____   ____   12. **Ten Seconds to Play!** When Chip Hilton
                      accepts a job as a counselor at Camp All-
                      America, the last thing he expects to run into
                      is a football problem. The appearance of a
                      junior receiver at State University causes
                      Coach Curly Ralston a surprise football prob-
                      lem too.

I have   I expect
read: to read:

____   ____   13. *Fourth Down Showdown:* Should Chip
                  Hilton and his fellow sophomore stars be sus-
                  pended from the State University football
                  team? Is there a good reason for their viola-
                  tion? Learn how Chip comes to better under-
                  stand the value of friendship.

About the Author

CLAIR BEE, who coached football, baseball, and basketball at the collegiate level, is considered one of the greatest basketball coaches of all time—both collegiate and
professional. His winning percentage, 82.6, ranks first
overall among any major college coaches, past or present.
His name lives on forever in numerous halls of fame. The
Coach Clair Bee and Chip Hilton awards are presented
annually at the Basketball Hall of Fame honoring NCAA
Division I college coaches and players for their commit-
ment to education, personal character, and service to
others on and off the court. Bee is the author of the
twenty-three-volume, best-selling Chip Hilton sports
series, which has influenced many sports and literary
notables, including best-selling author John Grisham.

more great releases from the

Chip Hilton Sports Series

by Coach Clair Bee

The sports-loving boy, born out of the imagination of Clair Bee, is back! Clair Bee first began writing the Chip Hilton series in 1948. During the next twenty years, over two million copies of the series were sold. Written in the tradition of the *Hardy Boys* mysteries, each book in this 23-volume series is a positive—themed tale of human relationships, good sportsmanship, and positive influences—things especially crucial to young boys in the '90s. Through these larger-than-life fictional characters, countless young people have been exposed to stories that helped shape their lives.

WELCOME BACK, CHIP HILTON!

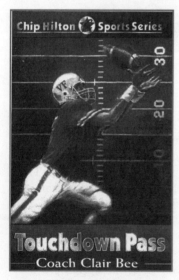

Vol. 1 - Touchdown Pass
0-8054-1686-2

available at fine bookstores everywhere